SCARY STORIES FROM MEXICAN GRANDMOTHERS

13 TALES FROM SOUTHWESTERN FOLKLORE

DIANE WILLSEY

KYDALA PUBLISHING INC.

CONTENTS

DEDICATION

For my students, who shared their stories and for my husband, whom I love, and for Ellie and Alice, the grandchildren I hope will share our stories someday.

Special thanks to John Hedtke for his inspiration, guidance, and encouragement.

PROLOGUE

MIJOS! Mijas! Come quick! I have found a very special present for you. It is a book, *un libro*, but not just any book. It is a special *libro*. You remember the old stories I tell you, the ones you laugh at when my back is turned? Well, here is a book that tells the same stories, the same *cuentos!* It is a book that comes from Mexican *nanas* like me. It tells stories from *sus familias.* And do you know what, my precious grandchildren, *mi nietos?* Many of these stories are nearly the same as the stories from *mi familia.* What did I tell you? *Sí*, it proves that the stories are true. You should listen to your *nana.*

Now read the stories, *mijos*. Listen close, *mijas*. I am your *nana*, your *abuela*. There are important lessons for you to learn.

1

THE CLUB DIABLO (THE DEVIL'S DANCE)

IT WAS DARK, very dark. Even the moon was hiding that night. I sensed that I ought to be hiding myself, but first I had to slip into the house without waking my parents.

They weren't going to be happy if they caught me sneaking in three hours late.

The house was as quiet as a morgue, but the front door creaked like the hinges on a coffin. Slowly, I pushed my way in. It seemed the slower I went, the louder the squeak became, so I finally just gave up and shoved the door all the way open.

As I stepped inside and turned to close the door, the hairs began to stand up on the back of my neck. Someone was watching me from the living room!

"And what do you think you are doing, Juanita?"

I nearly jumped out of my skin, but it was only my mother, waiting up for me. Why did she always have to sit in the dark like that? It was like she was waiting to ambush me.

"Mama, I'm sorry. I know I'm late but—"

"No more excuses. You are late again. You have no

respect for the rules of this house. This time you will go on restriction."

"Oh, no, Mama. Please, not restriction. I'll be good. I promise."

"You have been saying that for weeks, but you keep coming in later and later. It is time for you to pay for your behavior."

"But, Mama, tomorrow is the big dance at the Club Diablo in Nogales, remember? I want to go with Esperanza and Corina. Please, Mama. I have to go to the dance!"

"You should have thought of that before you stayed out too late. You will just have to miss this dance."

"But, Mama, I have to go. Couldn't I just start my restriction after the dance?"

"No more talk! I spoke to your father earlier. Would you like me to wake him so he can tell you himself?"

"No!" Of course I didn't want to face my father.

"Then go to bed. Your restriction will start now and will last for two weeks."

"Fine!" I stomped off toward my bedroom. What did I care if they put me on restriction? I was *going* to that dance, restriction or no restriction. Just wait and see!

I WAS AWAKENED THE NEXT MORNING BY POUNDING ON MY bedroom door.

"Wake up, Juanita! You are sleeping your life away!"
"Oh, Papa, leave me alone. I want to sleep in."

"You have slept long enough. It is time to get up."

"But, Papa, it's only eight o'clock. I need more rest."

"You heard me, *mijita.* Your mother has made for you a good breakfast. Then you can begin your chores for today."

Great. Not only was I on restriction, now I had *chores* to do, too. I could hardly wait. "Okay, Papa. I'm coming." Rolling out of bed, I rubbed my eyes and groaned. Man, this was horrible. What kind of life was this?

After changing into my Levi's and a T-shirt, I stumbled out of my room and down the hall. The aroma of *chorizo* and eggs drifted through the house, calling me to the kitchen table. I had to admit I felt hungry.

"I'm here, Mama."

"Good. Sit down and I will make for you a *burrito*. Do you want juice?"

"I guess. Uh...Mama?" "Yes, Juanita?" "Am I still on restriction?" "Yes, Juanita." "But, Mama—"

"No more talk, Juanita. Here is your *burrito*. Eat."

I poked around the flour tortilla with my fork. Man, this was bad. I had to figure out a way to get off restriction.

"Mama, if I do extra chores today, could I get off restriction?" "Juanita!" My father entered the room, and his big voice bounced off the walls. "Enough about the restriction. You know our decision. Now eat your breakfast. When you are finished, you can help your mother with the ironing. Do you understand?"

"Yes, Papa."

Great. Now I had to do the ironing. I hated to iron.

Nobody irons anymore. My family was from the dark ages.

I NEVER HAD SUCH A DAY. I KEPT LOOKING AT MY WATCH thinking that hours had passed when, in fact, it was only minutes.

It was torture, and my mood sank lower as the day progressed.

"Juanita, I think you have done enough for today," my mother announced at nearly five o'clock that afternoon. "You may now go to your room."

"Can I be off restriction?"

"Juanita, if you ask me that one more time, I am going to make it three weeks instead of two. Now go!"

"Fine. Just ruin my life. See if I care!"

I ran off to my bedroom before she could comment. I had some planning to do. There *had* to be a way for me to go to that dance!

I wasn't in my room more than two minutes when the phone rang.

"Juanita, it is for you," my mother called. "You may talk for ten minutes."

Gee, that was big of her. What good would ten minutes do? What could I possibly say to someone in only ten minutes? I muttered as I picked up the extension in my room.

"I got it," I screamed.

"Hi, Juanita. It's me, Corina." "Hi, Corina. What's up?"

"Well, are you ready for tonight? You know what I heard? I heard that Joey is going to be there. Isn't that great?"

"Corina, you are the one who likes Joey, not me," I grumbled.

"So what? You'll probably meet someone else there."

"If I go."

"What do you mean, 'if you go'? I thought it was all set."

"Well, I got put on restriction last night. I don't know how I can make it."

"Juanita, you have to go. It won't be any fun without you."

"Maybe not, but what am I supposed to do?"

"Why not just sneak out? I did that once. I waited until my parents were in bed and I went out the window. You could do it, too."

"Yeah, but if I get caught, I would be on restriction for the rest of my life."

"You won't get caught. Just take some pillows and towels and wad them up in your bed. If your parents look in, they'll think you're asleep."

"I don't know, Corina. It sounds a little risky."

"Well, do what you want, but I tell you what. We'll wait for you at the Circle K until 9:30. If you aren't there by then, we'll just go without you. Okay?"

"Okay. Listen, I gotta go. My mother is yelling. Maybe I'll see you later."

"Okay, Juanita. 'Bye."

I heard the phone click as my mother knocked on my door.

"It is time to hang up, Juanita."

"All right, already. I hung up," I shouted.

My bedroom door flew open. Papa was standing with Mama. "Watch yourself, young lady," he said. "You will speak with respect to your mother."

"Yes, Papa." Prison. This was prison. No privacy.

Ridiculous rules. No fun. I *had* to get out of there!

DINNER THAT NIGHT CONSISTED OF *ENCHILADAS* AND BEANS with *sopapillas* for desert. My throat felt like a clogged drain. I could hardly swallow a bite.

"Juanita, why are you not eating?" my mother asked.

"Because," I blurted out, "no one here cares about me or my life. I want to go to the dance!"

"Juanita," my father interjected, "we do care about you. In fact, even if you were not on restriction, we were not going to let you go to the dance. That dance club is not good for young ladies. No. Bad things happen in places like that."

"Oh, great. Now you're telling me that even if I'm good, I can't have a life of my own. Then what's the point? Why even try? I'm going to my room." I got up and threw my napkin on the table.

"You will not leave this table without permission," my father bellowed.

"Fine. Can I have *permission*?" I asked in my snottiest voice.

"Let her go, Gabriel," my mother said. "We have had enough for tonight."

My father glared at me, but he said, "Go to your room." I left without another word.

WHEN I TOOK SHELTER IN MY BEDROOM, I STARTED PACING and muttering, "Who do they think they are? They don't own me. I'm entitled to a life, too, aren't I? They don't understand me at all. They don't love me. They just want a slave." When I started talking to myself out loud, it became apparent that I was out of control. That's when I decided to follow through with Corina's idea. I mean, it was *my* life. I should be able to make my own decisions.

Sitting quietly, I waited to hear them go to bed. These old geezers usually went to sleep at nine o'clock. I supposed they wanted me to live like that. Well, no way. I was going out!

At 9:20, I was ready to split. The pillows and blankets had been strategically placed to look like a person in my bed. It didn't really look like me, but so what? They probably wouldn't check up on me anyway. They didn't care. All they wanted was to go to sleep and leave me in here to rot. Well, I wasn't about to do that!

Cautiously, I crawled through my window and out into the front yard. The pane opened right over some rose bushes, but I was watchful and avoided the thorns. Not wanting to snag my nylons, I stepped shrewdly, dodging the mud in the planter and avoiding the complete devastation of my only pair of black high heels. Vigilant, yes, but I still took time to check the window after I was out, making sure not to let it latch just in case I might decide to come back. After all, I might as well cover my bases and leave myself a way back in. That is, if I decided to come back. Maybe I would just stay out forever. That would show them, as if they even cared.

Within minutes I maneuvered my way through the hole in our fence and was on my way to the Circle K with no time to spare. When I got there, I was out of breath.

"There she is!" I heard Esperanza shout.

"Man, we almost gave up on you," said Corina.

"Hey, never give up on me," I mumbled as I fluffed my hair.

Corina gave my attire the once-over. "Wow. You look hot. That's a great outfit."

"Thanks. Well, what are we waiting for? Let's go!"

We hopped into Esperanza's old Plymouth and were on our way.

It took almost forty-five minutes to get to Nogales, and Corina talked about Joey for the entire trip. I could hardly take it anymore. "Corina, you got a sock?" I finally asked.

"What do you want a sock for?" she inquired. "To stuff in your mouth to make you shut up."

Esperanza laughed. "Take two. It might take that many to keep her quiet."

"All right," Corina pouted. "I'll quit talking about Joey, but why are you so grumpy?" she asked.

"I don't know. I just don't feel right about tonight. I guess I feel guilty for disobeying my parents."

"What's the matter, Juanita? You never cared about that before." "I know. I guess I'm just nervous."

"You'll get over it. Look, we're here!"

I glanced up and realized Corina was right. We had finally arrived at the Club Diablo. There was a funny feeling in my stomach, but I didn't want to spoil anything for Esperanza or Corina, so I just said, "Well, what are we waiting for? Let's go in!"

As we walked through the doors, it seemed like I was suddenly struck blind and deaf at the same time. I could hardly see anything except the flashing lights around the dance floor, and the music was so loud it sounded like noise, not music. I had to put my mouth right next to Corina's ear and scream to get her to follow me to a table. Corina then yanked on Esperanza's arm to get her to tag along.

We sat down on some red vinyl seats at a booth in the corner. The air was thick with smoke that hung like a heavy quilt over the room. When the waitress suddenly appeared out of the clouds, we ordered Cherry Cokes. I swear, I don't know how she even heard us over the music. It was sickening.

There was no use trying to talk. We just sat there, smiling stupidly. Finally, Joey walked up and asked Corina to dance. She was trying to act cool, but it was obvious that she liked him. When they got up, she nearly tripped as she ran out to the dance floor with him.

Next, Bobby, a friend of Joey's, asked Esperanza to dance. *Great*, I thought. *I'll probably sit here all night and never get asked.*

Just then, the most incredibly handsome man approached my table. He looked older and more sophisticated, so I thought he was going to just walk on by. Instead, he stopped and bent down to speak into my ear.

"Hello, *Señorita.* You look lovely tonight. May I ask for this dance?"

I couldn't even answer him. The shock of having a man, a good- looking man, ask me to dance was too overwhelming. Mesmerized, I simply let him lead me to the dance floor.

He was a magnificent dancer, whether he danced to slow songs or fast. His energy never ebbed; he never seemed to tire, and I didn't either. It was just too much fun being the center of attention. I could tell that every girl in the club wished she were me, especially Corina and Esperanza. That guy was simply fantastic. Feeling like a gorgeous princess, I danced with my prince, the most handsome man in the world. I was in heaven and this was the best night of my life, or so I thought.

Suddenly, there was a commotion near the door. I tried to look, but my dance partner took my face in his hands and said, "Do not worry, my sweet Juanita. Just dance with me."

Wait a minute. How did he know my name? I hadn't told him, so I was puzzled. Even so, I didn't think about it for long. Just being in his presence left me feeling hypnotized.

But then I heard a shout. "Juanita! Juanita!"

There was something about that voice. "Juanita!"

Unbelievable. Talk about embarrassing. The voice was my mother. What was *she* doing here? Good grief. This was great, just great. They must have figured out that I'd left, then they came looking for me. How excruciating. How humiliating. I wanted to crawl in a hole and die. That or throw up right on the dance floor. It couldn't be any worse.

"Pay no attention, *Señorita.* You have no need to worry.

You are with me now," whispered the kind stranger.

"I'm sorry," I answered. "You don't understand. That's my mother."

"I know who she is."

"Juanita!" my mother screamed again. "Look at his feet!

He is the devil! He has *chicken feet*!"

What? She had to be out of her mind, but I tried to look down at my partner's feet nonetheless. He covered them with his cloak.

"Why did you do that?" I asked. "What are you hiding?"

"Juanita!" my mother screamed. "Look in the mirror!

Look in the mirror!"

So I looked in the mirrors that hung on three sides of the club.

Suddenly, there were no red vinyl seats, no tables, no smoke. In fact, the room was completely empty except for me and my dance partner. My friends were gone, and everyone from the club had vanished. Then I realized where I was. I was at El Rio Ballroom, just three blocks from my house. I was totally confused and even more frightened. Where were my friends, the people, the music?

All that remained was my dance partner, who sneered at me, who snickered, "I hide nothing from my loved ones. I will hide nothing from you, my sweet *Señorita*. Go ahead. Look at me!"

"Oh my God!" I cried when I looked down. I couldn't believe my eyes. Mama was right. It was so *gross*. He had the feet of a chicken. I had been dancing with the Devil! As I tried to pull away, he held my arm in a vise-like grip.

I glanced back to the mirror. My partner, the handsome man, had disappeared just like my friends and all the people. In his place was the most hideous creature I ever imagined.

He was tall, I mean *really tall,* and he was bald with

pointed ears and skin like a bat, all wrinkled and shriveled. The chicken feet were still there, too. Frantically, I looked for the door.

"Where are you going, *Señorita?* Do you not remember?

You promised this dance to me."

My mouth opened to scream, but nothing came out. The devil, Lucifer himself, continued pulling me, yanking my arm nearly out of the socket. I was completely helpless. What was I going to do?

"Why are you struggling, *Señorita?"* he asked with a leer, eyes blazing red. "I thought you wanted independence. Come with me, and you will be free of your parents."

"I don't want to be free. Uh...uh...uh," I stammered. "I don't want independence."

Muttering, he forced me toward the rear exit. "Silly girl. I heard what you said. 'They don't love me. They just want a slave.'" He mimicked my voice perfectly. When I talked to myself earlier, it wasn't really to myself. The devil heard every word I had said. "Do not tell me you want to be their slave!"

"No.... I mean, yes.... No! I mean, I'm not a slave. I'm just their daughter!"

"You said they do not understand you. I will understand." "I don't want to go with you!" I howled.

Suddenly, from out of nowhere, I heard my Papa. "Let her go, Diablo! She is mine!"

The devil dropped his grip on my arm and disappeared for a split second. That would have been great if a huge black dog with red eyes hadn't taken his place.

"What? You say she is yours? I thought she chose to leave you. Is that not right, *Señorita?* Did you not say you were going to lead your own life?" growled the dog.

"Leave her alone, Devil. You cannot take her as long as I claim her."

In a split second, I knew what to do. Spying the door, I ran, and I mean fast, and headed toward my home. The Devil dog followed, but I had a slight lead. I could hear it breathing as it began to catch up with me.

Screaming, crying hysterically, I made it to the door of my house, which flew open. Papa grabbed my wrist. "She is mine, and I will never give her up!" Papa shouted.

"Are you willing to fight for her? Do you want to make a deal?"

"I have no need to fight or barter with you, Diablo. She is my daughter, my blood, *mi familia*. She has *not* forsaken me, but she *has* denounced you. You must leave her with me, and *you* will leave here alone!"

The Devil dog stared at my father, then slowly changed back into the image of my dance partner. Finally, he grimaced and turned to me. "*Sí*, I will leave alone, but I want you to remember me, *Señorita*, because I will remember you." He glared at me, and his eyes burned like fire through my skin. "El Diablo does *not* forget. El Diablo does *not* give up. El Diablo does *not like to lose*. I will just wait until next time. You will be back, am I not right, *Señorita?* Look for me. I will be waiting for you!"

Then I fainted, right into Papa's arms.

When morning came, I called Corina. She claimed that she and Esperanza had indeed gone to Nogales the night before, but I had never shown up. When I described the evening, I did so perfectly, according to Corina, even the part about her dancing with Joey. The only difference was that I had not been there.

I TELL YOU, *MIJITA*, THIS HAPPENED MANY, MANY YEARS AGO, but I remember it as if it were *ayer, sí*, yesterday. I want you to *recuérdalo*, to remember, too. *Sí*, I learned my lesson that night. *Nunca desobedezcas a tus padres*. Never disobey your parents. You, too, must learn from my mistake. Listen to your mama and papa, just as you pay attention to me. They love you and know what is best. You must never find yourself as I did, *bailando con El Diablo*, dancing with the Devil!

2

EL CUCUY (THE MEXICAN BOOGEYMAN)

EL COO-COO-Y

MY NAME IS ISABELLA, and I have a story I want to tell. This is important for everyone to hear, so I certainly hope you heed my advice. Listen. Pay attention and learn.

Sophia, my sister, was born three years before me. Sharing a bedroom with her was an adventure every night. When she was nine and I six, she could keep me laughing all night long. That was a problem, however, because our parents were not thrilled when we stayed awake and didn't go right to sleep.

It started innocently. We lay in our separate twin beds, and Sophia told me funny, made up stories. She could change a fairy tale into something truly outrageous and leave me in stitches, and "potty-mouth" stories were her specialty.

For instance, Sophia was an expert at "Goldilocks and the Three Bears," only her version was a little sick. It was perfect, though, for silly children who thought anything along those lines was hilarious.

"Once upon a time," she always started, "there was a girl named Dirtylocks. I swear, that girl never washed her hair, or her body, for that matter. She reeked."

My teachers would always wonder at my vocabulary. I was taught by the best, my older sister.

"Dirtylocks was sneaking around in the forest one day looking for animal scat, also known as poop, when she came to a rustic cabin with treasures inside, but no scat. Since her quest for animal droppings was a bust, she decided to go inside the cabin and explore.

"Once inside, Dirtylocks found a table set with three bowls—one tiny, one medium, and one very large. She looked inside and found...you guessed it, she found poop. Dirtylocks didn't think it looked too appetizing, but because she was so filthy, she didn't care. Sitting at a tiny chair in front of the tiny bowl, she couldn't even reach the bowl of poop. The obvious answer was to move to the second, the medium chair. Now she could reach the poop, but it was cold and hard and really didn't look edible. Having no choice, Dirtylocks moved to the biggest chair with the gigantic bowl. Well, this one was steaming poop, and a very healthy helping. The stench coming from the bowl was just gagging, so Dirtylocks decided maybe she wouldn't eat the poop after all.

"Instead, Dirtylocks went to the bathroom. The first potty was way too small, so she skipped it and tried the second. That one wasn't any better, so she hopped up onto the third, enormous commode and she..." There was a pause for effect. "She fell in! Yes, she was sitting with her butt deep in the toilet, and she wasn't the only addition to the pot. Yes, she had found her animal scat, but she didn't mean to sit in it!"

I'm sure you get the picture by now. Anything referring to excrement was hysterical to us, and we would giggle and cackle, sometimes actually falling out of bed. Our intent was to be quiet, but it never worked. Before Sophia could finish the story, we would hear footsteps in the hallway and scurry under the covers, pretending to be asleep.

The person who showed at the door might be our father, with his booming voice yelling, but most of the time it was our mother. Mama's voice wasn't as loud as Papa's, but she used a different approach. She would glare into the room and whisper, "Be quiet! Go to sleep! *¡El Cucuy te va a llevar!* El Cucuy is going to get you!"

Seriously, we really had no idea what she meant, but just to save ourselves from further hassle, we would quiet down and finally go to sleep, after just a few more snorts and snickers.

It was around that time that our parents purchased a new television and put the old family TV in our room. We were thrilled even though it was a big wooden box with dials and knobs and a black-and-white screen. Watching shows by ourselves was more fun, especially after we went to bed.

With the volume turned really low, we would watch, and of course, laugh and giggle. The rule was that we couldn't watch the TV after bedtime, but we always had to test commands. Every kid does.

There was just one problem with those old television sets. When anyone turned it off, it didn't respond immediately. Instead, the picture gradually faded away little by little. Even when it reduced to a tiny white dot, that dot would stay on the screen for an excruciating amount of time.

The TV was on my side of the room, so I was in charge of turning it off every time we heard one of our parents walking down the hallway. However, I could never turn it off fast enough. That tiny white dot would linger, and we would hear about it, for sure.

Our father had a very effective way of getting the point across when he knew we had disobeyed the television rule. Daddy would walk into our bedroom, take off his belt, and (wham!) hit the stool at the end of Sophia's bed. Great-grandmother Bisabuela had given us that stool, and it was ancient. Well, when Dad hit it, dust would fly everywhere in the room! For some reason, that dirty grit was scarier than actually being spanked, which Papa never did but we feared nonetheless. We always quieted down after that, and the television remained blank.

Our nighttime rituals were pretty consistent, but the entire situation started to become more complicated after a visit from our Nana and Bisabuela. Nana brought our great-grandmother for the visit, as she enjoyed going out even at her advanced age. Old or not, we adored both of them and looked forward to the time we could spend with them. Sometimes when they came, Nana would tell us stories and Bisabuela would try to interject parts. Our great-grandmother spoke only Spanish, but if she knew the story, she could contribute and Nana would translate. Of course, she always knew the legends, because the accounts had been passed from all the grandmothers in our family for years.

On one outing, Nana, Bisabuela, and Mama all chimed in. We had heard the threat of El Cucuy for years, but we didn't really know what it meant. That time, each had something to contribute. Apparently El Cucuy was a boogeyman who lived in your closet or under your bed. The monster would only bother children who didn't pay attention to their parents, especially those who wouldn't go to sleep when told.

To tell you the truth, I didn't really remember their stories, because we weren't actually listening. We simply enjoyed watching them get excited and use their hands and faces to get the point across. Later, I was sorry I didn't pay better attention.

After the visit, we were laughing and happy and had not a care in the world, at least until bedtime arrived. It was Sophia who wanted to watch television, but I, quite frankly, was too scared after the stories from that afternoon. I may not have paid complete attention, but I did know that the monster could come and get us if we didn't go to sleep. Still, my sister was quite bossy and used to getting her way, so the TV came on.

Not five minutes after our program started, Sophia suddenly sat straight up and whispered, "Did you see that?"

"What? You mean on the TV?"

"No, dummy. In the closet. There's something in the closet."

I looked toward the cubbyhole we called a closet, but I couldn't see anything.

"Do you see it?" Sophia questioned. "It is standing right there!"

She pointed to her side where her clothes were hanging. "Turn off the TV! Quick!"

"Okay," I responded. "I didn't want to watch it, anyway."

I went right to sleep after that, but I think Sophia had more trouble than I. She looked like she hadn't slept a wink when we were walking to school the next day.

"You didn't see anything last night?" she asked as we were slowly making our way toward school. "Nothing whatsoever?"

"You can ask me a million times, but the answer isn't going to change. There was nothing for me to see." I didn't say it, but I thought about calling her a scardey cat. Sensibly, I decided it wasn't worth the punch in the arm I would surely suffer if I did.

We went our separate ways once at the schoolyard, and I didn't see my sister until the afternoon when classes let out. It was apparent she still had El Cucuy on her mind, but when I asked, she just ignored me.

Bedtime seemed to come faster than usual that night. I

guess I was waiting to see what Sophia would do, but when it came time to crawl into our pint-sized beds, she had no interest in telling stories or watching the forbidden "boob tube" as my parents called it. Sophia simply went right to sleep, so I followed her example.

Our nights went on that way for a week. However, the more time passed, the less Sophia seemed to remember about El Cucuy. After ten days, she finally decided to tell me a funny poop story. I was happy to listen.

Unfortunately, the tale had just begun when suddenly Sophia repeated her actions from the week and a half before, frantically claiming that something was in her side of the closet. I looked again but saw nothing. Honestly, it just looked like clothes to me, but Sophia had bug eyes and appeared terrified so I simply said, "I don't want any stories tonight. Let's just go to bed." Patting myself on the back and thinking how mature I was, I stated, "I'm not afraid, but I want to behave. Go to sleep." Maybe being bossy wasn't so bad after all.

We fell into a deep slumber. At least, I did. As I think back, I guess Sophia appeared totally worn out the next day, so perhaps I should assume she hadn't had much sleep.

Not a word was spoken about the situation the next day, but we did go back to following our parents' directive that night. No stories. No TV. It stayed like that for a month.

After all that time, it was I who decided to take the initiative to go back to our ways. At bedtime, I turned on the TV. Sophia acted like she was having a heart attack, but I was brave and wanted to flaunt my new power over my sister Unfortunately, my bravery didn't last long after I looked at the closet. What I saw made me almost pee the bed. El Cucuy was there, with red eyes and jagged teeth, and he was staring at me! I nearly broke my arm trying to turn over so I could reach the knob and turn off the TV. There are no words to completely explain how I felt except to say that I knew I had made a mistake, a huge, gigantic, enormous blunder.

So there was only one action we could take. Screaming at the top of our lungs, we cried out, "Mama! Papa! Mama! Papa!" over and over again until both of our parents ran into the room in a complete panic.

"What? What? Are you hurt?" asked Mama.

"My God," shouted my father. "What in heaven's name are you screaming about?"

"El Cucuy!" we bellowed. "El Cucuy is in our closet. He is going to attack us!"

There was a glance between our parents that said something, but I didn't know what it was. It seemed that Papa was telling Mama what needed to happen without saying a word. She shook her head in agreement, sitting at the end of my bed. Papa returned to the living room.

Mama then rose to her feet and closed our closet door. Just sheltering our eyes from the garments lined on the hangers made me feel better. After the doors were secure, Mama put the footstool in front of them, effectively preventing any opening of the bifold entrance. Crazy, I know, but having those entrances blocked had an immediate effect on both Sophia and me. Mama stayed with us until we both fell into a troubled slumber, but a siesta nonetheless.

———

THE FOLLOWING MORNING, WE SLUGGISHLY READIED ourselves for school. Mama called us to breakfast, which we barely touched, and told us she had a solution to our problem and would take care of it after we took care of our education for the day. Without much confidence, we thanked her and started our meandering shuffle toward our destination.

Our path was lathered with danger. Sophia saw El Cucuy swinging at the park we passed along our way. I spied the beast on the bus that brought some of our classmates to school. We both saw the fiend on the playground when we arrived. Our nerves were shot, and we had no desire to enter our classrooms. Luckily, El Cucuy stayed away once we were inside, but we both were dreading recess and lunch and, well, the walk home. By that time, though, I was so upset that I began blubbering and sobbing that I couldn't walk home, even with my sister to accompany me, so the office secretary called home and Mama had to come pick us up.

I expected her to be furious, but she appeared more sad than mad. Looking at me, she softly sighed and said, "Stop your crying, Isabella. You are safe with me now."

"But Mama," we hollered, "El Cucuy followed us to school!"

"I told both of you I would help you this afternoon. You are going to be fine, because your Nana and Bisabuela are waiting at the house. They are experts and can deal with El Cucuy. Rely on them. Trust us."

What choice did we have? Sure, I saw El Cucuy sitting on the curb of the street, but I also felt better knowing I had Mama and, especially, Nana and Bisabuela. They were the three strongest women I knew. In fact, they were the toughest *people* I knew, male or female. If there was any hope, they were the ones who could conjure optimism. Knowing they were at my house made me more optimistic, at least a little.

Still, when we pulled into our driveway, I wasn't exactly ready to rush into our house. Apparently, Sophia wasn't either, but we both shifted through the front door to be greeted by the two women who loved us maybe even more than Mama. Both of the older and wiser women (Mama told us that) had obviously been awaiting our arrival. They jumped up to welcome us, even Bisabuela, whom I had never seen bounce up in any way like it. They took us into their arms, and for that moment, I felt completely at ease.

Of course, we all knew what was coming. Nana and Bisabuela sat us down and insisted we recount every detail of our encounters with El Cucuy. As they listened, each woman shook her head or whispered in Spanish to the other. Clearly they were paying very close attention.

As we completed our account, we were both exhausted, emotionally and physically. Tears began to well up in our eyes, and I felt a small stream run down one side of my face. Needing to feel loved, I climbed into my Nana's lap to feel her warm squeeze and cuddle.

We all sat quietly for quite some time, then my Bisabuela began to speak and Nana translated.

"Una vez que El Cucuy hace notar su presencia, es difícil, pero no imposible, despedirlo."

"Once El Cucuy makes his presence known, it is difficult, but not impossible, to send him away."

"Hemos tratado con El Cucuy antes, así que podemos ayudarte a deshacerte de este monstruo. No te preocupes."

"We have dealt with El Cucuy before, so we can help you rid yourself of this monster. Do not worry."

Reaching for their bags, each grandmother pulled out a vast array of religious artifacts. There were crucifixes, rosary beads, a prayer book and candles of the saints, particularly St. Agnes and St. Ursula, if I remember correctly. They picked these up and headed to our bedroom, pausing to admonish us to stay with Mama. We were not needed. Fine by us, of course.

Sitting, waiting, and worrying began to take their toll on

our minds. We were imagining every sort of scenario, and I truly worried for my grandmothers. It has to be one of the most nerve- wracking events of my life. I thought I was going to puke or faint or whatever happened when you can't take any more. The smell of candles burning was evident, and we heard murmurs of the Rosary prayers as well as other litanies. Evidently they were taking time to do the process correctly, whatever that procedure was. If I hadn't been so frightened, I might have dozed off, but I *was* scared so I just sat there, eyes wide open, and waited.

After what seemed like ages, Nana emerged from the room and asked Mama to retrieve the Holy Water she had received from relatives in Mexico. We stared at our mother with questioning eyes, but she offered no explanation. Instead, she entered the dining room and returned with a small, heavily packaged box. Opening it with a knife, she then withdrew a small capped vessel. As she removed the top, she made a nod to Nana.

Holy Water open and ready, we were told to enter the room, as it was now our responsibility to finish the process our Grandmothers had begun. Once inside, we stood at strict attention waiting to hear our instructions. Bisabuela was apparently in charge, because she spoke first and Nana translated.

"*Es hora de* bendigamos *con el Agua Bendita*."

"It is time for us to anoint you with the Holy Water."

Giving us direction, Nana then explained that Bisabuela was going to bless us and we were to repeat the Holy Water prayer when she did. So, as Bisabuela touched each of our foreheads, we made the sign of the cross and said aloud...

"By this holy water, and by Your Precious Blood, wash away all my sins, O Lord."

After that, we were told to kneel and pray to Saint

Catherine while Bisabuela circled the room and sprinkled Holy Water as she moved.

This time, Nana spoke, and we repeated the words line by line:

> "Glorious St. Catherine, help me to imitate
> your love. Give me strength and courage in
> fighting off the temptations of evil desires.
> Help me to love God with my whole heart.
> O St. Catherine, help me to be loyal to my
> faith and my God as long as I live. Amen."

At that, our grandmothers and mother knelt with us, and we all recited the Lord's Prayer. When finished, Bisabuela stood and spoke.

"*¡El Cucuy se ha ido!*" "El Cucuy is gone!"

We never saw the evil creature again, but, of course, we also never told nasty stories at night or disobeyed our parents when it came to going to bed at night either. Still, to this day, neither Sophia nor I will go to bed with a closet door open.

As children, if we forgot to close the wardrobe, we would cry out and one of our parents would come and shut the door, keeping that terrifying monster away. Today, I just make sure I never forget to do it myself. There is no use in tempting El Cucuy to return.

MIETOS, LISTEN CAREFULLY TO THOSE WORDS. EL CUCUY IS *malo, mucho* bad. *Si*, I have told you before. You must pay attention to your Mama and Papa. Go to sleep when they tell you. *Sigue las reglas*. Follow the rules. You do not want El Cucuy to come through your closet doors! *Él te atrapará!* He will get you, and I will cry if you are gone!

3

LA LLORONA (THE CRYING WOMAN)

(LĂ-YAH-R̂ŌNA)

Ms. Riggs was seventh grade English teacher in Marana, Arizona, just a few miles north of Tucson. Born and raised in the area, she was disappointed in herself for not knowing more Spanish than she did, which was very little. Even more amazing was that she knew very little of the Mexican folklore that was prevalent in the lives of her students. Determined to change that, she decided to ask her students for stories from their own families. She decided to get the ball rolling with the only story she actually knew, one that almost everyone had heard. It was the story of *La Llorona*, and this is the version she shared with her students.

It was dusk, and the sky was turning a deep mixture of colors as the young woman looked into his eyes. Those ebony globes held her entire world and were the deepest, darkest eyes she had ever seen. She adored them just like she loved him. He smiled at her, and she pulled him close. This adoration was amazing and wonderful and filled her with joy, something she had never felt before.

Gazing into that trusting soul reminded her of a day so many months before when Ricardo had been the man of her dreams. Young and trusting, she thought they were in love. Nothing could come between them. It embarrassed her to remember what she had done with Ricardo. Her mother would have been so ashamed! That didn't stop her, though, because Ricardo was everything to her. She would marry Ricardo someday.

Someday? It might have made her laugh if it wasn't so humiliating. That day never came. It couldn't, because when she told Ricardo of her pregnancy, he vanished completely, leaving behind the tiny village of their birth. Some friends shared that they heard he had gone to live with some relatives. Maybe, but all she knew for sure was that he left her alone to face the stares and the sneers. No one would stand by her side as she broke the news to her parents, which she never did. Instead, she had to hide her growing belly and was convinced she would become a stigma upon her family and herself. Therefore, since he left without a word or note or even a simple good-bye, she ran away, too.

Having no distant relatives to whom she could flee, she felt lost and very, very alone. With no idea where she might run, the poor girl couldn't even tell her family where she was going. She didn't even tell them she was leaving. No good-bye to her Papa; Mama left behind deprived of a kiss from her firstborn; a little sister without a hug from her older sibling. The disgrace was not to be shared. They would never know she was with child.

Of course, that was over nine months ago. Now she had a whole new set of problems.

Peering again into the dark eyes of her child, her son, she

saw the epitome of pure goodness, perfect in every way, yet grief overwhelmed her. Mama had never seen her first grandchild. Papa could not admire the baby's small but strong chin. The ache from the loss of her family gnawed at her very core. No good had come of any of this, except for the good that was her son. And now she had to end that, too.

She would have to drown the baby.

What else was she to do? She had no money or work, no place to live. Just this evening she had been forced to hide along the road in some bushes as *banditos* galloped by. Terrified that they would rape her then kill her and take her child to be sold into slavery, the poor young mother shivered in the shrubs. How could she let that happen to her beautiful baby? What else could she do to protect him? No choice. If she loved him, she must drown him in the river. There simply was no alternative.

"*Mijito*, I love you. I do not want to see you drown in the river, but I would rather you sink into the night than become a slave or prisoner of the *banditos*. You understand, do you not? I beg you, please do not hate me. Understand that I want only what is best for you."

She sat down at the river's edge and held her son close, singing to him a lullaby that her own mother had once sung to her. The baby cooed and laughed and tried to grab her face. She smiled as she sang, and then kissed him on the forehead. Stillness and silence finally engulfed them both.

"It is time, *Mijito*," she whispered. "Remember, I love you." She cautiously worked her way down to the edge of the river. After kissing the baby boy one last time, she closed her eyes, said a prayer, then held his tiny body below the water. As she counted to twenty, her body was motionless. Then her eyes opened.

He was looking at her! His eyes were open below the

water and he was looking right at her! Gasping, she let go of his tiny body.

The baby floated to the top of the river and was quickly carried downstream, bouncing over rocks and tumbling in the rapids.

The scream she let loose was the long, mournful wail of a mother who has lost her child. Rising to her feet, she started sprinting down the riverbank.

"Wait! Wait!" she cried. "Come back! I changed my mind. Do not leave me. Do not die. I love you. I want you. Please come back!"

Her desperate wailing and dreadful sobbing continued as she frantically ran down the river's edge, never catching up with her infant.

As soon as Ms. Riggs finished her version of this well-known tale, the students raised their hands, wanting to be called upon.

"That's not right!" shouted Raphael. "*La Llorona* is from Colorado, not Mexico. My grandma told me so!"

"No!" said Julia. "My *nana* told me she was from Old Mexico and she killed her three children to win the love of a soldier!"

"You're both wrong!" scowled José Luis. "My *nana* has seen her in Tucson, right next to the Santa Cruz River."

"That's crazy," declared Miguel. "The Santa Cruz isn't a river. It is a dry wash."

"You're the one without a brain," growled José Luis. "It hasn't always been dry. In fact, it still runs sometimes to this day!"

"Okay, that's enough," Ms. Riggs declared. "I know there are many versions. Why don't each of you go home and ask your parents or grandparents if they have ever heard the story? Since it's Friday, we can devote some time on Monday to hearing any editions you may hear from them."

The general atmosphere and response were surprisingly positive for students in middle school. Most of the kids couldn't wait to ask someone in the family. A few even shared that they would call their *abuela*, their grandmother, in Mexico. Even Ms. Riggs was enthusiastic about that. Anything that would motivate her students was a win, as far as she was concerned.

One of her students was a girl named Rosalie, who looked disappointed. After class, the instructor pulled the young woman aside and asked why.

"Ms. Riggs," explained Rosalie, "you may not know it, but I live in the middle of nowhere. I have to ride a school bus for an hour with my little brother, and we don't even have a phone. I don't know how I can ask any of my relatives."

"Don't worry," said her teacher. "Not everyone is going to be able to find stories. It's fine. You can skip this assignment."

Rosalie was very happy to hear that news. Normally, she would never want to skip any homework, but this time she just forgot about it. *La Llorona* didn't cross her mind again.

When Rosalie and her brother exited the bus that afternoon, they ran through their house, shouting to their mother to call them when dinner was ready. They had plans outside.

It was only a short time later that Ofelia, their mama, walked out on the back porch and called her children. "Chachito! Rosalie! Dinner is ready!" Chachito was a nickname that meant "little Chacho," which came from *muchacho*. The little boy was named after his father, who had passed away just a few years before.

"Aw, Mama. Do we have to come in now? We're building a fort!" whined Rosalie.

"You can finish your fort after dinner. Come in now before your food is cold."

"Okay, Mama. We're coming," Rosalie conceded. "Chachito, let's go. We can finish this later."

"But I'm not hungry. I want to stay out," whined her little brother. Chachito was three years younger than Rosalie, and sometimes she felt like his mother instead of his sister.

"Chachito, stop your whining. You heard Mama. We have to go in and eat now, but we can come back out after dinner. Don't make trouble. Let's go." Her brother could be a real pain sometimes.

Once they got to the house they sat down at the modest kitchen table and inhaled their dinner without tasting anything. They were in a hurry to return to their fortress. As the last bite was scraped from each of their plates, Chachito jumped up pushed his way to the back door. "Come on, Rosalie. Let's go."

"Did you forget something?" his mother asked.

"I'll put his plate in the sink, Mama," Rosalie volunteered. "I'll meet you out at the fort in a minute, Chachito."

"That is very kind of you, Rosalie. Chachito, you may go on ahead. Just be careful, and remember to stay away from the river."

"I'm always careful, Mama." Chachito let the screen door slam as he ran out. Ophelia just had to smile. So much like his father....

Rosalie gathered up the dishes and took them to the sink.

Though she did consider going right outside, she instead decided to help out by running the water and soap. "Heck," she whispered to herself. "I might as well wash them as well. Mama could use the help."

Fifteen minutes later the dishes were washed, dried, and put away. Ofelia thanked her daughter and then watched her gallop outside to find her brother.

As soon as Rosalie spied the fort, she gazed around the area. Chachito was nowhere to be seen. "Chachito! Where are you?" That kid was always causing trouble. Now where was he?

That's when she heard a high-pitched wail that sent chills up and down her spine. Looking around frantically for her brother, Rosalie was frightened, and wasn't even sure why. That sound was just so eerie, extremely creepy.

Another howl came, this time reverberating with pure desperation. That heartbreaking, overwhelming melancholy wasn't coming from Chachito. It sounded more like a mother pleading for a cherished lost child, but Rosalie's family lived out in the middle of nowhere. There were no other mothers besides her own in the area. And that was not *her* mother, she was sure. So who was it?

The mournful, gut-wrenching noises seemed to be coming from the river as they echoed around Rosalie. Panicking, she ran out beyond the cottonwood trees and scanned the area up and down the riverbank.

Then Rosalie saw a woman standing right next to the river's edge. She was pleading, beseeching, almost begging someone to join her. Those shrieks and the overwhelmingly mournful cries sounded so sad that Rosalie thought about joining the pitiful woman herself, but she wasn't calling to Rosalie. She was calling to Chachito.

Chachito was downriver on the bank. He was gazing at

the woman as if he were in a trance. The crisis intensified when as started walking toward the mysterious, shadowy woman.

Something is wrong here, thought Rosalie. "Chachito! Chachito!" She screamed for her brother like never before.

Turning partially, Chachito looked back at his sister with a strange expression on his face and a blank stare in his eyes. The young boy didn't even seem to see Rosalie.

The woman's cries became louder and more frantic. Paralyzed with fear, Rosalie felt she was glued to the ground. What did the woman want with her brother?

There was a sound from behind Rosalie. Whispering a slight "Oh!" Rosalie nearly fainted as her own mother rushed by her.

Ofelia was screaming, shrieking actually, as she flew by Rosalie and headed toward Chachito. "Leave my son alone, La Llorona! Leave my baby alone. He is my baby, not yours. Leave my son alone!"

Chachito seemed stuck between the two women, and each of them moved closer to him. Thankfully, Ofelia was the fastest, and she reached her son first.

Grabbing her boy in a vise-like grip, Ofelia sprang back up the riverbank. Once they were near Rosalie, the mother snatched her daughter's arm and nearly yanked it out of the socket as well. The determination she showed to get away from the river was superhuman.

It wasn't until they were safely in their own yard that Ofelia let loose of Rosalie's forearm and placed Chachito on the ground. Only then did her own sobbing begin. Looking exhausted, she sat down, right in the dirt, and started sobbing in a way neither of her children had heard before.

"Oh, *Mijito*. You scared me so much! Did I not tell you never to go close to the river? Have you not heard me say that you must stay away from there? *Mijito*, you need to listen to me! Never go back to the river! *La Llorona* is waiting there. She has been waiting for over a hundred years. Those cries are her way to call for her lost child, any child, even you or your sister! Please promise you will never get close to her again!"

It wasn't difficult for either Chachito or Rosalie to make that promise. The poor boy had eyes as big as cereal bowls and appeared to be close to losing his dinner. Rosalie didn't feel much better. They both swore they would never get close to the river again.

———

COME MONDAY MORNING, THE PLAYGROUND WAS BUZZING with tales from different families. By the time English class came around, some of the students could not contain themselves. They started sharing their stories even before the bell sounded.

"My *bisabuela*, my great-grandmother, said her own grandmother died just a week after seeing *La Llorona*," said Marina. "My mama says my *nana* still cries when she remembers, so I wasn't allowed to ask about the story."

"Well, I called my *nana* in Mexico," declared José, "and she told me that *La Llorona* killed her three children many years ago because her husband left her for a younger woman. The hope was that her husband would come back to her once she didn't have the burden of the kids, but instead of returning, he punished her by never speaking to her again. *Nana* says the woman became crazy."

The versions just kept popping up, and Ms. Riggs didn't put an end to them even after half an hour. When the room finally settled down, Ms. Riggs asked if anyone else had something to share.

That's when Rosalie slowing raised her hand and boldly declared that she had the best version to share with her class, because her experience was a first-person account. Everyone sat mesmerized as she explained what had happened. More than a few of her classmates were jealous, but Rosalie told them she would gladly have avoided the terrible situation had she been able. Of one thing she was sure—she and Chachito would never again play by the river!

Ophelia would later thank God her words were heeded. Forever after, she made the sign of the cross anytime she came near a river, any river, as did her children.

Mijito, REMEMBER THIS STORY WELL. *Si mi hermano*, MY

brother, was almost taken by La Llorona. It could happen to you. She is still there today, calling for her lost *niño*. She waits for children like you to come play by the river's edge. *No te acerquesa al rio*. You must stay away from the river. You must stay away from *La Llorona*.

4

EL CHUPACABRA (THE GOAT SUCKER)

BLANCA RUSTLED in her bed sheets and threw her soft, fuzzy blanket on the floor. With temperatures in the 100s during the day, a comforter on the bed was just too hot. Bedtime was hours ago, but she had awakened and couldn't get back to sleep. Such an aggravation. Her only comfort was that tomorrow was Saturday. At least there was a chance she could sleep in.

Wait. What was that noise? Oh yeah. Blanca knew that sound. Since her bedroom was just one wall away from the front door of their home, she could hear everyone's comings and goings. Glancing at her clock, she couldn't help but think, *What is Carlito doing coming in at this time?* Carlito was her teenage brother, a troublemaker in the family.

Blanca could hear him stumbling around making far more noise than usual. *What a jerk*, she thought. *He deserves to get in trouble. This would serve him right.*

Then, out of the blue, Blanca heard her father step into the hallway. Wow. Papa sure could yell when he was mad!

"Carlito!"

Blanca nearly fell out of bed, shocked by the volume and

intensity of her father's voice. "Carlito, what do you think you are doing coming home at this hour?"

Oops. Carlito knew he was in trouble. At least he ought to have known, but still he answered with a flippant response. "Why? What's it to you?"

Blanca actually hid under her covers waiting for her father's response. It wasn't going to be good, that's for sure. She couldn't actually see Papa's face, but she imagined it bright red and ready to explode even more. Holding her breath, she waited.

"Have you been drinking?" bellowed her father. "Have you been out in the desert? *What have you been doing*?"

"Only hanging out with my friends," replied Carlito, his words blurring. "I didn't do anything that the other guys don't do. Relax, Dad."

Blanca heard her grandmother, her *abuela*, come into the hallway. Abuela lived with them and always tried to protect the children. Tonight was no different.

"Carlos," she said to her son, Carlito's father, "now is not the time. Let us go back to sleep and deal with this tomorrow."

There was a long pause. Blanca had all sorts of thoughts running through her head. Carlito might be beyond help at this point. He certainly was asking for it.

Finally, Blanca heard her father mutter, "Go to bed, Carlito. We will deal with this in the morning."

There may have been some input from her mother, but Blanca was surprised not to hear more from her papa. She was certainly surprised he didn't react more, maybe with his belt. Blanca had never been spanked, but Carlito had met Papa's strap many times. Astonished that tonight wasn't another opportunity for the strap, Blanca instead heard her papa slam the bedroom door, Abuela quietly go back to her bedroom, and Carlito slither into his own room. Thank goodness!

Blanca hoped that would be the end to any disruption the night, but no. Instead, she was jarred awaked two more times by the sounds of her brother retching in the bathroom. *Good grief*, she thought, *he might puke all night*. Though Carlito was down the hall in the bathroom, Blanca found the echoes and odor made her feel nauseated as well. Ugh.

Then, at 5:30 in the morning, Blanca heard another sound. What was that? Her father was pounding on Carlito's door.

"Get up! You have a paper route. You need to make your deliveries!"

Okay, this is funny, Blanca thought. *Serves him right*. Carlito pleaded for mercy, begging for more time to sleep,

but none came. Papa made him get up, dress, and be ready to go, even if there was a decrepit stench coming from him. Vomit and liquor were not the best combination.

Papa took Carlito out and forced him to make his newspaper deliveries.

Blanca chuckled and went back to sleep.

THE WHOLE HOUSE CAME ALIVE AT 8 AM. MAMA AND Abuela made a wonderful breakfast that smelled like bliss to Blanca. Unfortunately, when Papa and Carlito came in from the deliveries, Carlito turned a strange color of green and ran to bathroom. The rest of the family enjoyed a scrumptious meal. Blanca fought off her laughter as she thought of Carlito. Blanca actually thought that was going to be the end of it, but after breakfast Papa went to Carlito's room and hammered on the door once again.

"Get up, Carlito! Take a shower. We are going to visit your *bisabuela*. Don't take too long!"

Blanca heard Carlito whine. "Why, Dad? I don't want to go visit my great-grandmother. She's okay, but she's so old. The whole house even smells like old people. Can't I just stay here and sleep?"

"Do you really want me to answer that?" sneered Blanca's father, his eyes narrowing into tiny slots no bigger than a coin edge.

Again, Blanca thought Carlito would get smacked, but he was lucky that time.

"Never mind," snickered Carlito. "I'll take a shower." Blanca snorted. This day was going to be a real treat,

mostly because it would make her brother so miserable. It brought a smile to her face. Seeing her brother suffer really was a pleasure.

THE DRIVE TO NOGALES TOOK ONLY NINETY MINUTES, BUT crossing the border took even longer. That's why Blanca knew this trip was important. Mama was never thrilled to wait in line at the crossing but rode in the back seat to keep Blanca and Carlito from squabbling. Abuela sat in the front passenger seat. Like most of her family, Abuela was from Old Mexico, and she was anxious to go back to her home country.

Blanca agreed with her mother. It was a hassle to go through the border with all of the delays, especially coming home when everyone had to show identification, but it was a pain with which Blanca could easily live. Her *bisabuela* lived with her daughter, Blanca's great aunt, her *tía abuela*, in Nogales, Sonora, just over the Mexican border. Though a small town, Nogales had plenty of attractions as far as Blanca was concerned.

Blanca genuinely enjoyed visiting the old county. Intrigued by history, she loved seeing the brightly colored houses and enjoyed the aromas that came from the different vendors selling what her father called "authentic Mexican food" right on the streets. Her mouth actually watered despite the fact that she was still stuffed from breakfast.

As they pulled in next to the bright blue house with the neon yellow flower boxes, Blanca grew excited. Before the engine of their station wagon was off, she burst from the car and ran to the door. She exploded into the house with a booming greeting of love and exhilaration, without even knocking. Blanca adored this house and everyone around it, in it, or even nearby. Mexico was heaven on earth, a beautiful paradise for everyone.

Blanca was greeted in much the same way. Being the only granddaughter (and great-granddaughter) to the women she adored gave her a special place of honor. How much fun it was to feel that boundless, overwhelming adoration. She could only sigh with deep satisfaction as she hugged her *bisabuela* and *tía abuela*, her grandmother's sister, with sincere affection. Can anyone really explain the love of a grandmother? Blanca's *abuela* was overcome with joy as well. She had not seen her mother or sibling for a long time. Blanca saw tears roll down Abuela's cheek.

Blanca's parents, with Carlito trailing behind as slowly as a sick snail, entered the house soon after. Even amidst the delight of the greetings the women had for the family, Blanca could tell they were extremely concerned about Carlito. It was scary, even to Blanca.

After greetings of affection and hugs all around, Blanca heard her father ask her *bisabuela*, his grandmother, something in Spanish. By the look on his face, she knew it was time for her to "go outside and play." If she was sneaky enough, she just might be able to stay close enough to the door to hear what they were going to say. Declaring her intention to play outside, Blanca let the screen door slam as she ran out into the yard.

Back indoors, the family started a conversation that Carlito was not particularly happy to hear, but Blanca knew that he was kept in his chair by their father's glare. As Bisabuela only spoke Spanish, her daughter, Abuela, translated for him. Blanca, standing close outside so she could hear and actually watch much of the action, knew Carlito wanted to roll his eyes, but she was also keenly aware that Carlito recognized that the backhand of his father's fist would follow, so he kept quiet and tried to keep any emotion from showing on his face. Of course, Blanca was smiling ear-to-ear.

One sentence at a time soon grew into long, quickly recited information. From the best Blanca could hear, the story went something like this:

"Recuerdas, Mija," began Bisabela. *"Cuando eras una adolescente y esos chicos malos a quienes creías tus amigos."* The oldest woman spoke to Blanca's father.

"You remember, *Mija*. It was when you were a teenager and, how you say, uh hanging with those bad boys you called your friends," translated Blanca's abuela while glaring at Carlitos.

"Te lo había dicho y te había dicho que te quedaras en el interior para no entrar en el desierto."

"She told your father again and again to stay indoors, to not go into the desert."

"Eso fue por lo que había ocurrido en mi pueblo cuando era una niña pequeña."

46

"That was because of what had happened in her village when she was a small girl, a very young girl, younger even than Blanca."

The words began to flow like a river and sounded like a flood rushing past. Blanca could hardly keep up with both grandmothers.

"El origen de nuestrafamilia se remonta a la gente Jakalket y vivió en las estribaciones de las montañas Cuchwmatan en el noroeste de Guatemala. Mi abuelo trasladó a la familia a Coatzacollos, México, 'El lugar donde se esconde la serpiente.' Este es el lugar donde Quetzalcoatl hizo su último viaje al mar hace más de mil años. Coatzacollos era un lugar difícil para le sobrevivencia de familia, así que el padre de mi madre se trasladó todo el norte al pueblo de Huaulta de Jiménez, Oaxaco, México. La familia comenzó a criar cabras por su leche. Vivieron allí muchos años antes de que comenzaran los problemas. De hecho, ese era el pueblo en el que nacimos nosotros dos, tu tía abuela y yo."

"Our family dates back to the Jakalket people and lived in the foothills of the Cuchwmatan Mountains in northwest Guatemala. Mi abuelo's grandfather moved the family to Coatzacollos, Mexico, 'The place where the snake hides.' This is the place Quetzalcoatl made his final journey to the sea over a thousand years ago. Coatzacollos was a difficult place for the family to survive, so my mother's father moved everyone north to the pueblo of Huaulta de Jiménez, Oaxaca,

Mexico. The family began to raise goats for their milk. They lived there many years before the problems began. In fact, that was the pueblo in which both of us, your *tía abuela* and I, were born."

At this point, Blanca simply had to tune out her great-grandmother, her bisabuela, and just listen to Abuela.

"The terror began when your great-grandmother was a small child. She heard terrible screaming from the herd of goats. Terrified, she scurried to tell her mama. The screams had come very close to where your *bisabuela* had been. Her mama, my *abuela*, sounded an alarm and everyone ran as fast as they could to find the animals. When they arrived, many of the goats were dead and all of the blood had been sucked from their bodies.

"This happened many times as the years passed, and not just to our family. It happened to other *familias* as well. Every occasion began with ghastly screams and ended with many goats dead with no blood. Some people were able to see the creature doing these evil deeds. They described it as walking on two feet with spikes on its back and long, sharp teeth. A name soon followed: El Chupacabra."

At this point, Blanca realized that her *bisabela* had actually stopped speaking. Her *abuela* was simply going through the tale from her own memories.

"When I was born, I knew little of these happenings. My mama and papa were very careful with me, though. It was a rule that I could never be out of their sight, but one time when I was about *cinco*, oh I mean five, years old, I decided to have an adventure. I wandered off and began to pretend I was an *exploradora*, an explorer. What fun! But I didn't watch the time, and the darkness began to fall. That was when I heard those dreadful cries. I, too, started my own ear-piercing screams and headed home, running and crying, nearly frightened to death! When I finally arrived at our home, the look of terror in my parents' eyes told me they had been very worried. Both of them grabbed me and hugged me and started talking very fast. They told me of El Chupacabra, the goat sucker. I had nightmares all night!

"In fact, my nightmares continued for weeks, and that is when my papa decided he was no longer willing to put his family in danger. Papa told everyone, including *tias* and *tios*, aunts and uncles, that we were moving to America. That is why we came to this country, and why your papa and you and Blanca are Americans. You are so lucky." Taking a breath, she glared at Carlito.

That pause gave Blanca her chance. "What about mama?" asked Blanca, who had finally given up with pretending to play outside. "Did she know about El Chupacabra?" she called through the screen door.

"*Sí.* My family was with your father's *familia* when we came to America. Your father and I were born in Arizona as well," replied her mama, "and we knew El Chupacabra very well."

"I am tired now," Abuela interjected, "and I think the stories are upsetting your *bisabuela*. Perhaps we should go and your father can tell you the rest of the story on our way home."

"There's more?" exclaimed Carlito and Blanca at the same moment. However, Blanca was thrilled; Carlito was not.

"Yes," replied their father. "There is more, but your *abuela* is correct. We need to start home. Let's get to the car." Kisses and hugs were exchanged, for the most part anyway. Carlito thought he was too old for that, but their papa insisted he say good-bye and thank his great aunt and great-grandmother. Blanca did it with love and without prodding.

When they finally managed to settle down in the automobile, Blanca was ready to hear more. Jumping up and down, even though she wore a seat-belt, she begged her father to continue.

"I am a little tired," grumbled her papa. "Let's make it through the border crossing before I say anymore."

There was no use in arguing, so Blanca began to relax and melt into the seat. Once they were at the crossing, the tempo of the car (slow, very slow) and the rhythm of the engine (not much faster) lulled Blanca into a light slumber. It might have occurred to her that the nap was her father's intention, but she was too tired to notice. She fell deeper and deeper into dreamland…

WAIT! AS SOON AS BLANCA REALIZED THEY WERE MOVING again, she became wide awake. Sensing the situation, though, she decided to stay quiet and act like a slumbering baby. A shrewd smile crossed her lips.

"Carlito, I am going to finish the story of El Chupacabra, but I want you to listen, not speak. It is not easy for me to share, so please stay silent."

Carlito nodded to show he understood, but his expression didn't seem very interested. Blanca, silent as a saguaro in the desert, was ecstatic.

"When I was about your age, I started to make friends with some boys who were not the best influence. Of course, it is easier to blame them than take responsibility for myself.

"We lived in Picture Rocks. Do you remember visiting there when you were younger, Carlito? It is just a small community west of Tucson."

Again, it was easily apparent that Carlito wanted to roll

his eyes. Instead, he spoke up and said, "Can't you just call me Carl like my friends do?"

Well, that did it. Carlos began to pull the car off the road. Blanca figured her papa was ready to use that belt and use it well.

"No, please don't pull over," Blanca's mother and grandmother said at the same time. "Please."

"Alright, I will not pull the car to the side of the road, but one more interruption, and I promise you I will, Carlito! I am tired of your mouth."

The story continued. "I was out with my friends in the desert."

"Why were you in the desert?" asked Blanca, forgetting that she was trying to pretend to be asleep.

"When I say no interruptions, I mean no interruptions from *anyone*. Have I made myself clear?"

Blanca and Carlito were smart enough not to answer aloud. They just nodded vigorously, making sure their father saw their response.

"I assume you are not speaking to me with that statement, my son," said Abuela. "I assume you know *not* to talk to me that way."

The kids' mama actually burst out laughing, but no one else dared make a peep.

"Of course, not, mama," said Carlos. "I would never speak that way to you."

"And never like that to your wife, either. Am I right?" "Of course, Mama. Never to either of you."

Blanca was surprised her mother could stifle her snicker, but she did.

"Good. Now I can return to the story. One night we were in the desert *drinking beer,* when we suddenly heard hideous, unbearable screams. We could not tell if the shrieks were from a predator or victim, or maybe both. We just knew that *something* sounded like death, and horrifying demise at that."

"You were old enough to drink?" asked Carlito, forgetting not to interrupt.

"No! I wasn't old enough! But I thought I knew everything, as my son does today," yelled Carlos.

"What happened next?" inquired Blanca, also forgetting. After a short glare, Carlos continued. "We were too stupid to admit we were terrified. Instead, we decided to check out what was going on. As we moved silently through the desert, we came closer and closer to the brawl.

"Just when we were almost upon it, we suddenly saw a silhouette in the moonlight. It was easy to figure out what was happening. The shadows spoke, and we saw a huge creature using some sort of small animal as a toy that was about to be torn apart. It was hard to actually know *what* we were seeing, but when we saw the shadow seem to turn and look at us, *that* we understood.

"We ran, and I mean we zoomed across that desert landscape as fast as rockets. Yes, it was hard because the desert was so dark, but that didn't stop us. From somewhere in back of us, we could hear the snorts and growling as some sort of weird animal was chasing us, and it was catching up!

"We continued our pace all the way back to Picture Rocks, splitting up only as we neared our homes. The creature was almost upon us when my friend Javier jumped into his yard.

"Unfortunately, my house was the farthest away, so I was the last to reach safety. Just as I turned at our street, I felt hot breath on my neck and then a scratch on my back. Even though I was wearing a coat, the claw of the beast was able to bring blood to my backside. Luckily, I still had a bottle of beer in my hand. I threw it behind me without even stopping or eyeing what it was attacking me. I was just too freaked out.

"Thank God I had that bottle and was able to distract my assailant. Judging from the horrifying sounds behind me, I could tell the monster had fallen behind ever so slightly. The grunting and shrieks from our hidden assailant never stopped until I reached home, hurried inside, and slammed the door."

"I was worried, very worried," Abuela interjected. "That's why I was waiting up for your father."

"And I thank the Lord she was there, because no sooner had I sat down to tell her what happened, we heard a noise that was the most terrifying commotion I have *ever* come across. I had no idea what would make those sounds until your *abuela* figured it out. That's when she screamed out....

"Of course I screamed! It was El Chupacabra coming in the cat door! It was coming for both us! So I grabbed your father and ran to my bedroom and locked the door behind us!"

"What happened then?" Carlito asked. Finally, he had become interested in the tale.

"We heard the creature get stuck in the cat door," replied Papa. "The screaming turned different. Hard to describe, for sure. It just sounded so *angry*! We could hear El Chupacabra thrashing around, trying to get clear of the door, but it couldn't make it into our home."

"But I don't understand," whispered Carlito. Raising his voice slightly, he asked, "How do you know it was El Chupacabra if you never actually saw what it was?"

"Because the next morning we found our cat, *el gato negro*, dead in the front yard. All the blood had been sucked from his handsome black body. When I picked him up, he was like an empty sack. It truly was hideous."

Abuela continued right where Carlos left off. "We also

found that each of the families from the boys who had been in the desert had suffered the loss of an animal. One lost a cow, another a horse, and almost every dog in the neighborhood was dead. How did they die? Each had been sucked dry of blood!"

"Oh my God!" said Carlito. "It could kill animals as large as a horse or cow? That means it could easily kill a human!"

"We were safe, but your father was lucky. He could have died that night, and he could have caused *my* death," said Abuela. "And there would be no Blanca or Carlito."

Both of the kids' faces were chalk white and their eyes were huge, round, and looked ready to pop out of their heads. "Enough of this," declared their mother. "No more in front of Blanca!"

Blanca wanted to protest, but the truth was that she was terrified, so she really didn't mind. By the looks of Carlito, she thought he didn't either. They both had learned a lesson, that was for sure.

The desert, especially at night, never looked the same to them again.

MIJOS! MIJAS! DO YOU UNDERSTAND? MY BROTHER, YOUR *Tío Abuelo*, could have died! That is why I worry so when you want to go out at night in the desert. Please, *por favor*, do not make my heart give out. Do not wander in the night! Do not go into the desert! El Chupacabra lives there still and will come for you as it did Carlito. I do not want to lose my grandchildren, *mis preciosos nietos*, to the Goat Sucker.

5

LA MUJER DE BLANCO (THE WOMAN IN WHITE)

THE FACTORY WHISTLE screamed the end to another workday. Tomás threw his gloves into his locker and picked up his lunch pail. His friend Armando slid in next to him and started to open his own locker.

"Hey, Armando! What do you say to a drink? Shall we stop at Rosa's Bar on the way home?"

"I do not know, Tomás. The last time we went for a drink, I could hardly get you to leave. I do not want to stay out late. Emma and the kids will be waiting for me."

"Don't worry. I don't want to stay late, either. After all, my wife and children are waiting, too."

"Yes, but you leave them alone more often than I do, Tomás. I do not like to stay away. I want to spend time with my family."

"Well, we can still stop for one drink. If you are worried about leaving, we can take separate cars. I have my truck today. You have your car, do you not?"

"Yes, I have the car. I just don't know."

"Whatever. I don't want to twist your arm. I can go without you." Tomás was beginning to feel offended.

"No, no. I am sorry, Tomás. I do not mean to sound like I did. I would love to go for that drink. Are you ready?"

"Ready as ever!" answered Tomás as he slapped Armando on the back. Both men headed toward their vehicles. "I'll meet you there!"

Rosa's Bar was less than a mile from their job. The place was right off the main road, but it was not exactly well known. It was a pink, cinder block building with no windows in the front or on the sides. *Rosa's Bar* was painted in black script letters above the door on the west side. Not exactly elegant, but it served its purpose. Tomás arrived just ahead of Armando. He waited beside his red Chevy pickup while his friend maneuvered into a tight spot.

"Be careful, Armando! I wouldn't want to see you scrape that lovely paint job of yours!"

"Thank you, Tomás. I appreciate your concern."

It was a joke between the friends. Armando's car looked exactly like the vehicles in the junkyard down the street. Tomás doubted if Armando would even notice if his car was scraped. That was why he teased. Armando could take a joke. He was a good friend.

The friends headed into the dark bar. They had to stand just inside the doorway for nearly thirty seconds before they could walk in further. Eyes adjusting to the light, or lack of it, inside the bar the friends were soon able to make out the shapes and faces of the other patrons. They moved slowly along the bar and found two open seats.

Climbing up on the rickety stools, Tomás greeted the bartender and shouted, "Jose, my friend! How are you this fine evening?"

"*Muy bien, Señores*. What can I get you?"

"I'll take a beer, on tap," replied Armando.

"Me, too. And give me a shot of Cuervo Gold. You want a shot, Armando?"

"No, Tomás, I told you I will not be staying long, did I not? I will just have one beer with you."

"Suit yourself. Just bring me a shot, Jose, and don't forget the lime and salt."

"Comin' right up." Jose walked down the bar to retrieve their drinks.

The bartender returned in a moment with two glasses of beer and a shot of tequila. He placed the alcohol in front of Tomás and Armando and quickly grabbed the salt shaker and a handful of lime sections. "Anything else, *Señores!*"

Tomás shook his head to indicate that they didn't need anything. Jose grabbed a twenty-dollar bill off the bar in front of each man and went off to get their change.

"*Salud*, my friend," Tomás said. He shook some salt onto his fist, then licked it with his tongue. This ritual was followed by an immediate downing of the burning liquid. Two seconds later, the glass drained, he squeezed the lime and stuck it between his teeth. His face contorted with the mixture, but he was soon smiling at his friend. "Great stuff!"

"I would prefer to slick with beer. Tequila is too strong for me. No, I do not want to get drunk tonight."

"Well, it's not too strong for me. Jose! Bring me another shot!" Tomás waved at the bartender.

Jose walked up and stated, "*Señor*, I have not even had a chance to bring you your change from the first round! Give me a moment and I will return with another shot." He turned to Armando. "Anything for you?"

"No, *gracias*. I will just drink this beer and then I will be heading for home."

Jose dropped Armando's change in front of him, removed the money for the second shot from Tomás' money, and then left his change as well. Within a minute he returned with Tomás' second shot.

"*Salud*," Tomás uttered as he raised his glass to Jose. After following the usual ritual, the second shot went the way of the first. "So, how have you been, Armando?"

Armando noticed that Tomás' words were already beginning to slur. He winced to think of his friend getting drunk and making a fool of himself, but he knew better than to try to talk him out of it. Tomás did not like to hear criticism of his drinking. It was better just to ignore it and leave as soon as he could.

Armando tried to engage in a polite discussion, but Tomás ordered another shot, and then another. By that time, intelligent conversation was impossible. Armando decided it was time to leave.

"Good night, my friend," he said to Tomás as he rose from his bar stool. "My wife is waiting, so I have to go. You should think about leaving, as well. Do you not think it is about time?"

"You go on ahead, Armando. I will soon be on my way. I just want to stay and keep Jose company a little longer."

"Well, drive careful, Tomás. You have had much to drink."

"Don't worry about me. I can hold my liquor."

Armando could hardly understand his friend. It was if his mouth was stuffed with cotton. Still, he did not want to start an argument. After patting Tomás on the back he headed out of the bar.

Stopping just before he pushed the heavy door to the parking lot, Armando heard Tomás strike up a friendship with the woman who had been sitting near them. Speaking to himself, Armando muttered to himself, "Just mind your own business." He pretended not to notice the flirtation, silently slipping out the exit.

Tomás spent the evening as the life of the party. He talked and joked, played pool and danced, and, of course, he drank. The one thing he didn't do was check the time. Hours flew by like a movie on fast forward.

"*Señor*, it is time to go. Will you be all right to drive?" asked Jose.

"What? Why is it time to go?" inquired Tomás. "The bar is closing, *Señor*. You will have to leave."

"Oh, sorry. I guess you are right then. I'd better get moving."

"Are you able to drive?"

"Yeah, sure. Don't worry about me, my friend. I'm good to go." Tomás staggered toward the door with a couple of other bar closers. He knew he was a little unsteady on his feet, but he eventually made it to his truck. Struggling to fit his key into the ignition, he ultimately made the engine turn over. Slowly, like a caterpillar moving across asphalt, the vehicle somehow emerged from the lot.

Not five minutes later, Armando returned to Rosa's. Walking through the threshold, he spotted Jose cleaning the bar.

"I am sorry, *Señor*," said Jose. "The bar is now closed."
"Pardon me, Jose. I was just looking for my friend,

Tomás. His wife called me asking me to check on him. Poor woman. She is sick with worry."

"Well, you just missed him. He left about five or ten minutes ago."

"*Gracias*. Jose. Forgive me, but I must ask. Was he drunk?"

Jose confirmed Armando's suspicions.

"Well, I will just drive toward his house to make sure he

arrives safely. Thank you, and good night." Armando headed for the parking lot and within minutes was on the road to Tomás' house.

Tomás was on the road, too, but just barely. He could hardly see the lines on the pavement. Grateful that the traffic was light, he still didn't feel bad enough to pull over. All he had to do was just concentrate, and soon he would be home. Just concentrate…and drive slowly, very slowly.

Tomás looked ahead on the road and held the steering wheel tight. Not much farther. Then he saw something up ahead and slowed down. What was it?

The truck headlights made contact and it was then that he realized it was a woman standing beside the road. She was clothed completely in white, and the beams from his lights seemed to illuminate her entire being. Coasting by before he could think, an idea popped up in his head.

Quickly applied his brakes, Tomás grabbed the wheel, cranked it to the left, and made a U turn in the middle of the street. Reversing his path, he was able to stop when he was across from the woman.

"Hey, *Señorita*, do you need a ride?"

The woman nodded in response. Yes, she needed a ride.

Tomás whipped the truck back around in the opposite direction and pulled up alongside the woman. "Get in. I'll be happy to take you where you are going." The woman opened the truck door and hopped up on the passenger seat, but she did not look at Tomás. As he had seen, she was dressed all in white in a gorgeous long dress made of lace. Her head was covered with a white shawl. He wanted to see her face.

"Señorita, where can I take you?" Tomás asked, waiting for her to turn toward him.

The woman's gaze did not falter from straight ahead. She raised her hand and pointed down the road.

"Well, I understand if you are the quiet type. You just keep pointing and I will take you where you want to go." Tomás smiled to himself. *This night might turn out to be something really special*, he thought.

As Tomás continued to try to make conversation, the woman acted like she didn't even hear him. It didn't bother Tomás at first, but before long he started to feel strange about the situation. Why wouldn't she talk? Who was she? Where was he taking her? It was no use asking. She wouldn't answer.

The drive was becoming uncomfortable. Tomás decided that maybe he didn't want anything special to happen with this woman. Maybe he just wanted to go home. Right in the middle of his thoughts, he suddenly felt a tap on his shoulder. He turned to look, and there was the woman in white looking straight at him.

She has a skeleton face! Tomás was petrified. He screamed in pure terror as she raised her hand and touched his forehead, slowly caressing his face. It was almost too much for Tomás, and the thought of dying crossed his mind. For the first time that evening, he thought of his wife and how much he truly loved her.

The Skeleton Woman smiled, showing the face of a death mask as she grabbed the wheel. Her long bony fingers wrapped around the mechanism and cranked it to the right.

The last image etched in Tomás' brain a huge oak tree. The truck barreled toward as if shot from a gun across the pavement. *Why is my foot on the gas pedal?* Was his last thought before the vehicle slammed into the tree. Unable to make sense of the situation, Tomás lost consciousness in the collision.

Luckily, Armando rounded the bend not two minutes later. Stopping his car, he jumped out to help his friend.

Frantically yanking the driver's door to the truck open, he pulled Tomás from the wreckage. Another car came by soon after, and they raced Tomás to the hospital.

Emergency personnel worked on Tomás throughout the night. If it hadn't been for Armando and the other driver, Tomás would not have lived. Lucky for him they came along and his injuries were tended.

———

THE NEXT DAY, THE POLICE CAME TO INTERVIEW TOMÁS. They asked him to explain the circumstances of the accident. Unfortunately, he was still nearly incoherent, so there was little they could do. They stopped in the hall after the interview and spoke to Armando.

"Are you the friend who found him after the accident?" they asked.

"Yes, it was me," replied Armando. "Can you tell us what happened?"

"I did not see the accident, but I must have come upon it right after it happened. I do not know why he hit the tree. There was no reason for him to turn to the right."

"Did you by chance see anyone else with him in the truck?"

"No, of course not. Why do you ask?"

"Well, he is pretty hard to understand, but he seems to be trying to tell us about some woman in white. Do you know anything about her?"

"No, officer. There was no woman in white when I got there. I am positive. Perhaps it was just a, how you say, a hallucination."

"Maybe so, but he seems pretty adamant. I guess we had

better check the area just in case. Sometimes people are thrown from the vehicle in a crash like this."

As Armando entered Tomás' hospital room, he thought he saw a movement at the window. He walked over and looked out. Nothing was there except a woman in a white dress walking away, but she was across the courtyard. Watching her for a moment, he realized there was something odd about the way she moved. She didn't seem to walk. It was more of a gliding action, like ice skating with fluid movement. Sunlight seemed to sift right through her body.

Armando watched the apparition as she moved out of view. Closing the curtain, he whispered, "I guess now I am hallucinating." Moving a chair next to his friend, he began the long wait for Tomás to awaken.

The police reported back later that afternoon. The woman in white was never found.

You see, *Mijo*? You see what can happen when you spend time at the bars? My brother, Tomás, nearly made the biggest mistake of his life. That is why he no longer drinks the alcohol, no. He does not go to bars and he learned to *apreciar a su esposa*. How you say? Oh, I know, appreciate his wife. It was she who *lo hizo bien otra vez*, made him well again. Tomás is a better man because of this, but he does not want you to go through what he did. No. He told me to tell you the story. *Sí, él quiere que estés a salvo*, he wants you to be safe. Learn from his lesson, *Mijo*. Do not go to bars or drink alcohol, no, and stay away from *misteriosa* women. One of them just might be *La Mujer de Blanco*, the Woman in White.

6

LA MANO PELUDA (THE HAIRY HAND)

ALEX SLAMMED the screen door as he stomped into the kitchen. The temperature outside was almost as hot as his anger. *What a bunch of jerks*, he thought. *There's nobody around here worth being friends with. They're all creeps.* The kids at Alex's new school were nothing like his friends from back home. Imagine, these bums had dared to tell him he wasn't welcome in their group if he acted like a bully. *Well, who needs them anyway?*

As he opened the refrigerator, Alex reached for a bottle of cola. There wasn't even anything good in there to eat. He was sick and tired of this whole place.

Two minutes later, Alex's sister, Maricela, bustled through the door with one of her friends.

"What are you two snot-nosed twerps doing here?" Alex asked as he pulled Mari's braid. "I don't want you in here. Get out before I get sick."

"Leave us alone, Alex!" Mari cried. "We're not doing anything to you."

"You live don't you? That's doing something to me. It's bugging me and I want you out of here!"

"Come on, Lupita," Mari said to her friend. "Let's just go in my room and get away from Alex, the bully. Then we can tell Mama when she gets home."

Lupita nodded as they rushed from the room, while Alex laughed and pointed at them. "Twerps! Babies! Brats! Go ahead. Run away. Tell Mom. Who cares?"

Once they were gone, Alex didn't feel much better, but at least he browbeat them to get his way again. It was better than nothing, he decided. And if his mother tried to get involved, he'd just tell her off, too. Sick and tired, yes, he was sick and tired of everything and everyone.

Mrs. Morales, Alex and Mari's mother, drove up into the driveway twenty minutes later. She honked the horn, hoping that Alex and Mari would hear her and come out to help with groceries. Keeping her eye on the kitchen door, Ophelia found no one came to her rescue. "*Supongo que,*" she muttered. "*tendré cargarlo sola.* I guess I will just have to carry them in myself." Thankfully, just as she opened the back end of the station wagon, Mari and Lupita came scrambling through the door.

"Sorry Mama. We were in my room and had to put the dolls away before we came to help. Should we grab a bag?" asked Mari.

"*Muchas gracias, Mijitas.* Thank you for the help. I am very tired. Where is Alex?"

"He's sitting in the living room watching TV," whined Mari, "and he's being mean to us."

Ophelia shook her head. "I am sorry, girls. I do not know what is wrong with Alex lately. He seems upset all of the time. Just try to stay away from him, *por favor?*"

"It's not just us Mrs. Morales. Alex is mean to everyone," tattled Lupita.

"Well, I will try and talk to him," answered Ophelia, balancing one bag of groceries on her hip while turning the doorknob of the screen door. "I guess it's time I put an end to his bullying."

Lupita and Mari smiled at each other at the thought of Alex getting in trouble. "It serves him right," whispered Lupita.

"I know," agreed Mari. "But I still wish he would just be nice."

When they walked through the door, the girls saw Mrs. Morales unpacking the groceries. "Alex?" she called. "Alex! *Ven aquí.* I need you in here, please!" She continued to unpack the bags, but there was no response from Alex. "Alex! Are you in the living room? I need you in here, *ahora mismo*, right now!"

"Hold your horses. I'm here already. What do you want?"
"Could you please get the rest of the groceries out of the car?"

"Why can't you ask the two little rats?" he asked, looking at Mari and Lupita. "They aren't busy. I'm watching my favorite show."

"Alex, every show is your favorite show," answered his mother. "I need the groceries right away. I do not want the milk to spoil. Please get it now."

"Well, that figures," complained Alex as he headed toward the door. On the way, he pulled Mari's braid and stuck his tongue out at Lupita. They both started screaming.

"Alex, you do not behave like that," his mother said. "Stop it, please."

Alex ignored her and went out to get the rest of the groceries.

"Lupita and Mari, I think it's time you went outside to play. Go out in the backyard and play on the swing."

"Ah, Mama. We don't want to go out back. Can't we just stay inside?"

"Maricela, I said to go out back. I do not want to hear any more about it."

"Okay, Mama. We'll go." The girls headed for the backyard just as Alex came through the door.

"Great. I have to work, but they get to do whatever they please. Just like always."

"Alex, what is bothering you?"

"Nothing is bothering me. I just hate living here. I just hate this stupid house. I hate my stupid little sister and her stupid little friend. I hate my stupid school. I hate this town, and I hate you, too!" Alex exploded.

"Alejandro Morales! You watch your mouth, young man. You do not know the trouble you can cause!"

"Why should I even care? Nothing matters to me. I hate everything, especially you!"

"That is enough. Go to your room without any supper. You have no right to talk to me that way!"

"I have all the right I need. If you don't like it, why don't you send me away?"

"I said that is enough. Now go to your room!" "Whatever!" Alex wasn't about to let her have the last word. He stomped out of the kitchen and down the hall to his room. "And I don't want any of your crummy cooking anyway!" he shouted as he slammed the door. He quickly opened it once more, poked his head out, and yelled down the hall, "And I still hate you!" Then he slammed the door a final time and plopped down on his bed.

"I hate them all," Alex whispered. "I don't care what they do to me. I hate them!"

A<small>LEX AWOKE WITH A START</small>. I<small>T WAS LATE, AND THE HOUSE</small> was quiet. *Great,* he thought. *I can get my own dinner.* He rolled off the bed and went to the door. He grasped the door handle, but it wouldn't turn. Confused, he tried again and still was unable to leave his room. *Man, she locked the door. Usually it only locks people out, not in. I can't believe it. She locked me in my room! Well, fine. I don't need dinner anyway!*

He reached up and flicked off the light. *I'll just go back to bed. So what? I don't care at all!*

As he slowly made his way back to bed in the dark, Alex sensed something strange on his foot. *What the heck is that?* he thought. *I almost tripped over something. It felt like it had a hold of my foot!* He felt around with his toes, but found nothing within his reach. *Geez, I must be going out of my mind. I better get back in bed.*

When Alex got to his twin bed, he crawled out of his pants, slipped beneath the covers, and stretched out on his back. *I don't need anyone or anything. I'm just going to get some rest.*

Closing his eyes, Alex tried to get back to sleep. Just as he was about to drift off again, he felt something tug on his blanket. Whatever it was seemed to have caught his cover. He tugged, and it came free. Turning over and over, he finally settled into the same position on his back, and closed his eyes.

Wait! He felt it again. *What was that?* Something was actually pulling on his blanket! Alex kicked his foot and tried to shake it off. *What could this be? We don't have any pets. What is pulling on my blanket?*

Alex tried to kick again, but he felt the thing pulling itself up along the edge of his cover and became paralyzed with fear.

"Mama!" he croaked. **"Mama!"** There was no answer. She couldn't hear him from her bedroom at the other end of the house.

Now the anomaly was on his leg, crawling along his blanket. Alex wanted to shake it off, but he couldn't move. All he could do was lie and wait as he felt the odd, indescribable "thing" make its way up his torso. Crawling slowly, at a snail's pace, it moved along the blanketed highway of the young man's torso. Alex heard what appeared to be the sound of fingernails scratching their way along his blanket. *Good Lord,* he thought. *What is it?*

Finally, the aberration reached Alex's stomach. As the moon shone through the window stretching across his body, the creature crawled into the light. *What is it? It looks like a big hairy hand!* The hideous fist stopped on Alex's chest, and, if it had eyes, Alex would've sworn it was staring at him. The stench of the sickening extremity with its moldy and decaying skin nearly made Alex puke as it started moving in circles. When the motion finally halted, the grotesque limb began flexing its joints up and down on his chest. Alternating between digging its nails into his blanket and relaxing its digits, the ghastly form crept closer and closer to Alex's head.

Then it jumped and landed right on Alex's face! He felt it sit there for a moment. Gagging, Alex could smell its perspiration and felt the hairs on the hand rub along his skin. *Oh my God! Is this hand human or animal?* Alex honestly couldn't tell. When he tried to open his mouth to scream, the hand smothered his cry with its damp palm. The disgusting odor was overpowering, and Alex's arms seemed glued to his side. Unable to move, he was trapped like a frightened rabbit in a snare. There was no way out.

THE HAIRY HAND BEGAN TO TREMBLE. ALEX FELT THE CLAW-like fingernails slowly tearing and digging at his face. Then he felt blood run down his cheek as the hand dug deeper. That was the last thing he knew before he passed out.

THE NEXT DAY, ALEX AWOKE TO A PILLOW COVERED WITH blood, hair, and a smell he couldn't describe.

Thankfully, there was a knock on his bedroom door, and h ismother entered a few seconds after.

"Oh my goodness!" cried Ophelia. "What has happened to you? Why did you not call for me?"

Alex could barely speak, but he had enough sense to apologize to his mama. He wasn't sure why, but he had a whole new attitude. No more hateful remarks were going to come from his mouth, that was for sure. That was a night he never wanted to relive, and he didn't.

Mijito, have you seen Josie's Tío Alex, her great uncle? You have seen his face with all the marks?

That is how his face came to be so scarred. It was his own fault, because he was so mean to others, *sí*, but mostly because he told his dear, sweet mother that he hated her. So you listen *Mijo*. Do not ever treat your mother with disrespect, and never say you hate her. Your face is perfect. It is young and smooth. We would not want *La Mano Peluda*, the Hairy Hand, to change you the way it changed my friend's poor brother, Alex.

7

BLOODY MARY

MICHAELA SHUFFLED along the dusty road as she walked to her bus stop, her lack of enthusiasm apparent to anyone who might cross her path.

Though a beautiful young woman, Michaela's face was a portrait of agony. It was the first day of school, and even though she was a junior in high school, it was also her first time to walk to the bus stop.

There had been no reason for Michaela to take a bus ever before. The schools she attended were all in her neighborhood. That was, however, no longer true. Something called desegregation came along, so instead of walking the three blocks to her old school, she now had to walk nine blocks to a bus stop. Not only did that not make sense, but it would ruin her life, at least in Michaela's view.

Last month, forty students were chosen at random to attend a different, more modern high school miles across town. To add insult to injury, as far as Michaela was concerned, she was the only junior chosen. No seniors were in the group, either, as they were allowed to stay to graduate.

That meant Michaela had no friends with whom to share this torture.

As she reached the bus stop, Michaela found that the other teenagers looked just as distressed as she felt. The largest group consisted of twenty-five freshmen, or so she heard. That seemed to be an accurate count. *Poor kids*, she thought. They seemed like kindergarteners, each on the verge of crying. Not that she didn't feel that way herself. Putting on a brave face, she was determined to hide her secret feelings that could only be described as dread, anxiety, even panic. What a crappy way to start her junior year.

Once loaded on the bus, the trepidation of Michaela and her refugee comrades didn't fade. Even when the vehicle pulled into the unloading zone, she still felt like she was in a nightmare from which she couldn't wake. When the group exited, an assistant principal greeted them with paper maps explaining the layout of the campus and answering questions on where they needed to be.

Then one of the freshman boys bent over and puked right there in front of everyone. Even the experienced student council members who had gathered to form "buddies" with the newbies had to stifle their laughter. Michaela thought she might just get back on the bus and pretend nothing happened. Maybe she could get a ride home. No luck. She and the others were guided off to start their day while "Vomit Boy" (as he soon became known around the campus) was escorted to the nurse.

Michaela's "Buddy Helper" was named Rachel, whose long, flowing, blonde hair was in direct contrast to Michaela's short, curly black locks. Their clothes were quite diverse as well. Rachel wore a crop top and really tight jeans. Michaela's mother would have had a coronary if she had ever tried to slip that outfit by and go to school. Instead, Michaela wore a bulky hand-me-down dress that fell past her knees.

There was no way she was going to fit in. Mama had left specific directions with her to be optimistic. Well, Michaela was positively negative about this experience already.

Rachel appeared kind, but Michaela caught her rolling her eyes to some friends many times that morning. There was nothing for Michaela to do but follow along and keep her head down. Crap. This year would be torture.

When lunchtime came, most students went through the cafeteria line or headed to the snack bar where they could purchase candy, soda, and premade sandwiches. As for Michaela, she took a brown bag out of her backpack and started eating her peanut butter and honey on a bagel, normally one of her favorite choices for the noon-time meal. Today, she felt conspicuous. Everyone was watching her, or so she thought, and when she produced an apple from her stash, Michaela actually heard students snickering, and her thermos brought outright laughing. Evidently, canned soda was the refreshment of choice, and Michaela felt like a strobe light was reflecting off her milk container.

Thankfully, when finished with their meals, the students could exit out to the patio. Michaela was so upset she threw the rest of her lunch away, emptied her drink, and almost ran to the open space known as the courtyard.

She hoped to be less conspicuous once she could mingle with others, but, of course, Michaela didn't blend in. Her clothes were just another beacon inviting attention that was not even close to hospitable. Boys called her "Grandma," and girls labeled her dress as "high fashion" in such a sarcastic tone that it made tears well in her eyes. She felt like a kindergartener.

As a last resort, Michaela ducked into a restroom and

barricaded herself in a stall, planning to stay there for the rest of the day if she must. Instead, Rachel showed up and coaxed her out and on with her day of classes. Michaela certainly didn't trust her "buddy," but decided that skipping class would gain her even more undesirable attention, and she certainly didn't want that! It was better to just plod along and make it through the afternoon. She counted the seconds to the end of this wretched day.

When the last school bell sounded, Michaela wanted to sprint to the bus, but instead, she walked as calmly as she could, hiding the tears in her eyes. The only word she could find to describe her day was "miserable," but she had to plan her story with better adjectives. Mama worked two jobs, and Michaela knew she would ask how her first day had gone.

Thankfully, Mama didn't return home from her duties until after 9 p.m. so there was time for planning. What Michaela didn't have was time to think before she would see her *nana*, who lived with her and Mama. Nana would ask questions, and Michaela had to be ready with a few "white lies." The family had enough worries without adding school woes to the pile. Michaela would just keep those to herself. Hiding her feelings was nothing new.

By some sort of miracle, Michaela made it through her first week without alarming either her *nana* or mama. Nothing changed, however. The other students made fun of her, and she felt totally isolated. Miserable didn't even come close to describing her mood or situation. Filled with melancholy thoughts, there was no way out. For probably the first time in her life, Michaela understood the phrase "grin and bear it." That's what she had to do.

The status quo did not improve with time. After twelve weeks of the school year had passed, Michaela saw no change, and she felt like she didn't have a friend in the world, let alone around campus. Her depression worsened by the day, week, and month. The notion of skipping school raced through her mind many times, and her grades began to suffer. Not sure how long she might have to endure this torture, it was becoming quite obvious that if her life continued on this path, she might not even graduate. Her Mama and Nana would keel over should she drop out or fail, so she tried to maintain and make it through the agony. "Never surrender" became her mantra. Too bad it was easier said than done.

As October ended, Michaela finally saw a glimmer of hope. Rachel, her "buddy" from the first day, actually began to talk to her without a snide tone. Not to say that everyone followed that example, but slowly some of Rachel's other friends began to appear to accept Michaela as well. It wasn't that they seemed overly friendly or kind, but at least that group stopped their abuse. If they were to treat her indifferently, that was fine by Michaela. At least they weren't battering her with insults.

By the final week of the month, there were many conversations about parties and costumes. Michaela wasn't a part of those discussions, but she heard them anyway. Halloween was not big on Michaela's hit list anyway. So what if she wasn't invited?

Shockingly, on the Monday before the big holiday, Rachel and her friends, Ellie and Melissa, approached Michaela and invited her to a sleep-over! The plan was to go to Rachel's house Friday evening and have the entire night for fun, and the best part, according to Rachel, was that her parents would be out of town. No meddling from adults. It was a dream come true, again in Rachel's perception.

As for Michaela, she was simply happy to be invited to anything, so she accepted even before asking permission. That, like so many other characteristics, was unusual for

Michaela, but she blew it off. It was more important to get invited to a party than to dwell on trying to receive Mama's approval. If she missed this party, there might not be any future invites. Nope. Michaela wouldn't let that happen.

When Friday morning came around, Michaela wrote out a very explicit note for Mama and Nana. It detailed her plan of attending the sleepover and noted Rachel's address and phone number to ease their minds of any trepidation. No, she hadn't asked for permission, but she did know that giving the details was a responsible action. No good could come from panicking the adults in her life by just not coming home from school. That would be crazy, of course.

Michaela stuffed a change of clothes and her pajamas into her backpack and left her home with the usual good-byes. The note was placed on the dining room table where Mama and Nana couldn't miss it. Trustworthy and conscientious, Michaela thought. Those were her middle names.

For the first time that entire semester, Michaela found herself excited to go to school. She could hardly wait for her classes to end. That was when she and the other girls would walk to Rachel's house and have a great time. Michaela was sure of it.

AT THE BUZZ OF THE FINAL BELL FOR THE DAY, MICHAELA rushed to meet the others in the courtyard. When she arrived, Rachel and Ellie were already positioned at the gate. They all waited patiently for Melissa, who arrived two minutes later. Once assembled, Rachel called, "Follow me!" and they were off to her house, just a short distance away. Each of the girls chattered like clucking chickens, even Michaela. The night was starting off perfectly.

Less than five minutes later, Rachel announced that they had arrived. Michaela almost choked when she saw the size of the house. It was a massive piece of architecture, probably five times the size of Michaela's home, and that was only the first floor. Suddenly, doubt crept into her mind, and she felt terribly out of place. Luckily, no one seemed to notice, so the initial panic subsided, and she began to fill with excitement once again.

Of course, that only lasted until the girls walked through the front door. *Oh, my God!* thought Michaela. *I've never seen anything even close to this place! Just look at the furniture! See the size of the living room, and look at the paintings on the walls! Oh, my God!* A running conversation trampled through her brain, and she seemed to have no control over it. With every room, her self-conversation gained even more momentum. Unbelievable.

When Rachel finally introduced them to her bedroom, Michaela almost fainted. In her family, ten people could have slept there, but here it was all for Rachel. Again, just preposterous.

"Hey guys, throw your stuff on my bed," commanded Rachel. "We'll go to the kitchen and find a snack."

Michaela tried to calm herself as she imagined the kitchen would be just as shocking as the other rooms in the house. She wasn't wrong. The kitchen brought out a gasp from Michaela, and Rachel looked at her with a puzzled face.

"What is it, Michaela? Haven't you ever seen a kitchen before?" quipped Rachel. The other girls laughed, but it didn't seem unkind, so Michaela just relaxed and giggled with them.

"I was just wondering how a beautiful, thin young woman like yourself could ever need as much food as there must be in that refrigerator. Good grief. You could feed an army!"

Michaela was pleased with herself for the flattery she gave Rachel, and Rachel seemed just as delighted. Rachel appeared to grow an inch, standing straighter even while laughing.

"Don't be silly," Melissa chimed in. "Rachel can eat anything and everything and never gain a pound. I wouldn't be surprised if she empties the fridge before the night is done."

"I just hope she leaves a bite or two for the rest of us," offered Ellie. "I'm hungry, too." It became a contest to see who might give the biggest compliment to their hostess.

And so it went for hours. By the time the sun was retreating to make room for the moon, the girls decided to order pizza and have it delivered. Rachel's parents had left her money to cover expenses, or so she said. Michaela caught a glimpse of five or six twenty-dollar bills. That could buy an enormous amount of pizza, for sure. They even ordered a dessert pizza, which was a new concept for Michaela, but something with which each of the others were quite familiar. All three assured her that she was in for a colossal treat.

They didn't mislead; that dessert was a S'mores pizza that consisted of tons of chocolate, marshmallow, and who knew what else. It was to die for.

I'm having such a fabulous time, thought Michaela. *This might be the best night of my life.*

After stuffing themselves with pizza, Rachel had a new idea. "Let's play make-up!" she declared.

"What's make-up?" asked a puzzled Michaela.

"Good grief, you know what make-up is," chided Ellie. "We're going to use cosmetics and be stylists for each other!" added Melissa.

"Oh," whispered Michaela. That was fine, but actually she wasn't allowed to wear make-up. Still, what could it hurt?

"Let's head to my mom's bathroom. That's where she keeps her best supplies," declared Rachel. "This is going to be fun!"

When they entered the master bath of the house, again Michaela couldn't believe her eyes. *You could fit twenty people in here*, she thought. Starting to say it out loud, she stopped herself because she didn't want to sound like someone from another world, though that's exactly how she felt.

Like an all-female pack of dogs, the girls descended on Rachel and began applying every cosmetic they found. Matte foundation, black eye liner, two-coat mascara, cheekbone rouge, smoky eye shadow, and anything else they could find. They successfully kept Rachel from seeing herself while they worked, so that the finished version was a "reveal" like they had seen on television. When the troupe turned Rachel around, she gasped. Everyone knew she was beautiful before the make-up, but now she looked like a model, truly extraordinary.

"Me next! Me next!" cried both Ellie and Melissa. "I want to go next."

Rachel had a plan. "Okay, Michaela you take care of Ellie. I'll do the work on Melissa. Let's get going and see who looks the best when we're done."

Michaela felt disadvantaged as she had no other experience with makeup other than what she had just learned, but she bravely went to work on Ellie. Thankfully, Ellie was already quite pretty, so Michaela knew she couldn't do much harm.

Michaela finished first but kept Ellie waiting to view the outcome until Rachel completed the job on Melissa. Both guinea pigs were turned to see themselves at the same time.

Though not as dramatic as the reveal for Rachel, both girls were pleased. Melissa was relieved.

"Now it's your turn, Michaela," announced Rachel. "Sit right over here."

Michaela noticed some sort of exchange between the others. Nothing was said aloud, but she was convinced they communicated with their eyes. *Oh well,* she thought. *I might as well give it a try.* She sat down as instructed.

The pack fell into place once again with Rachel taking the lead. While they worked, something struck them as funny. Michaela had no idea why, but the girls were burst out with laughter every once in a while. Just when her suspicions became upsetting, the girls swung her around.

What Michaela saw was amazing, yes—amazingly hideous. The girls had covered her face in thick foundation and over applied everything else. The result was something out of a horror movie, and Michaela began to cry.

Just as incredible was the response from Ellie and Melissa. They seemed very apologetic, sympathetic, and even a little embarrassed for their actions. Ellie quickly grabbed a wet towel and began removing their work of Halloween art. Melissa helped and repeatedly begged Michaela not to cry. Both offered to redo the job after they had removed most of the make-up, and even though Michaela quit crying, she politely refused to allow them to apply anything again.

Racheal was pretty much silent during the whole affair, but she did offer a cursory apology to Michaela. In truth, the request for forgiveness didn't seem very sincere. There was obviously something more on her mind, though she didn't say so right away.

Twenty minutes later, they found out what Rachel had been planning. "Let's go play with the Ouija Board!"

Michaela had no idea what she was talking about. "What

is a Wee-Jee Board? I've never heard of it. How do you spell it?"

Ellie explained, "It's where you can talk to the dead. You ask them questions, too."

"It's spelled O-u-i-j-a," added Melissa.

"Talk to the dead?" Michaela seemed uninterested in the spelling then. She was much more concerned with the prospect of the supernatural inquisition of long-passed souls.

"Don't be scared," quipped Rachel. "It's stupid but also fun. Let's go get it from my room."

Michaela wasn't as thrilled as the others, but she followed along anyway. Still stinging from the make-up incident, she was so desperate for friends that she felt pressured to stay silent and shadow the group despite her earlier humiliation.

The girls clustered like cackling geese, as they retrieved the Ouija Board from Rachel's room and headed straight to the dining room. Michaela felt like the Ugly Duckling, deliberately following behind. Queasy feelings in her stomach made her question the whole adventure. Yet, she still tailed the clique and ended up at the table with the rest.

Once seated, Rachel coached her little ensemble to sit close so everyone could lay their fingers on the small, plastic "portal," as she called it, that would act as a bridge to the "other side." The overall tone was very somber and somewhat gloomy. Michaela didn't see how this was going to be fun, but, of course, she didn't utter a word.

Bossy Rachel instructed everyone to sit and stay absolutely silent to allow the "spirits" to contact the girls. Following her orders to the letter, the room fell still and quiet. They waited.

Suddenly, the portal began to slide. Michaela's eyes grew wide as she and the others watched the movement around the Board. Every time it paused, the girls called out the letter on which it stopped. Finally, they understood the first message.

I am here, said the Ouija Board.

"Who is here?" asked Rachel, like she was expecting the question. "What is your name?"

The portal on the Ouija Board started moving again, letter by letter, and spelled Bloody Mary. This time, everyone except Rachel looked like her eyes would explode.

"Oh my God," whispered Melissa. "I'm going to hurl."

"Why?" asked Michaela. "Who is Bloody Mary?"

"She lives in the bathroom mirror," explained Ellie. "She is evil."

The portal moved again, spelling, *I am not evil*.

"That's not what I heard," said Melissa, while Ellie nodded in agreement.

Rachel hadn't said a word, but the portal moved again.

Come see me, it said.

"No way!" shouted Melissa and Ellie in unison.

Please, replied Bloody Mary.

Rachel jumped up and made a decision. "We're going to the bathroom," she ordered. "Everyone follow me!"

This time, the followers were much slower to react.

"Hurry up!" screamed Rachel, so they did, despite the reservations.

Back in the master bath, Rachel explained that they would shut the door and turn off the lights. When their eyes had adjusted, they would face the mirror and call for Bloody Mary together. After three invitations, she should show herself.

"Seriously," whimpered Ellie. "Do we have to do this? I really am scared."

Melissa and Michaela nodded in agreement, but Rachel ran the show, so she shut the door and dowsed the light.

Standing in front of the mirror, Rachel paused for about twenty seconds to let their eyes ready themselves for the lack of light. Then she started chanting, very slowly, "Bloody Mary."

Pause. "Bloody Mary." Another pause. "Bloody Mary."

Then it happened—the face of a torn, scarred woman pulsing with blood showed itself in the mirror. "Happy to see you," said the apparition.

That was all it took. All the girls, even Rachel, jumped and then dashed out of the bathroom as fast as they possibly could. Just outside the door, one of them tripped. The Ouija Board was right there, as if waiting for them.

"Who put this here?" demanded Rachel. No one would take credit. "Fine. I'll just put it away." She ran to the dining table, retrieved the portal and the box, returned to her room and put the Ouija away in her closet.

At that, they all returned to the dining room. The Ouija Board was once again on the table.

"How did you guys do that?" questioned Rachel. This time, there seemed to be more confusion and doubt, but she gathered the board and portal once again and returned them to her room.

The others waited in the dining room. When she returned, they decided to grab something to eat from the kitchen just to settle themselves. When they entered the pantry, there sat the Ouija once again.

All four girls screamed.

Michaela was the first to actually speak. "We have to burn it," she pronounced. "We have to destroy it."

Surprisingly, everyone agreed, even Rachel. They gathered up the parts, along with lighter fluid and matches, and headed to the backyard. Once there, each girl gathered leaves and twigs to kindle the flames. Placing all of it atop the board, Michaela lit a match. With a sizzle and a spit, the fire burned, and the girls watched the Ouija melt away.

Back in the house, Michaela announced that she had experienced enough. She was going to call her mother and get a ride home. Melissa and Ellie asked if they, too, could get a ride with her mom. Michaela said she would ask.

"What about me?" screamed Rachel. "I don't want to stay home alone!"

"Then come to my house," offered Ellie. "You can stay with me."

Visibly calmer, Rachel agreed. Michaela called home, apologized profusely, and begged her mama to come rescue them. Though it was late, and she was tired, Mama agreed and showed up at the door forty minutes later. Nana was in the auto as well.

Surprisingly, Mama didn't ask many questions. She simply deposited the girls at their homes (Rachel with Ellie) and started toward their own house on the other side of town.

Once they had the car to themselves, Michaela began to tell Mama and Nana everything that happened that night. Mama didn't even have to ask. Both women just listened as Michaela went on and on, terrified even after it was over.

"You are lucky, *Mijita*," Nana finally said. "That Ouija Board is not gone. I promise your friend will find the Board again. *Sí*, and the Bloody Mary, she is not gone. No, she is still in the mirror."

Mama nodded in agreement. "And I guarantee that if you or any of the other girls *ever* call for Bloody Mary again, in *any* mirror, she will come. But next time, she will take you with her. Make a vow, right now! Tell me you will not do that."

Michaela made the pledge easily. She had no desire to go through another night like that again.

Afterwards, Nana asked, "Will you tell your friends the same?"

Both women were surprised to see Michaela falter. There was obviously something more on her mind.

It was then or never. Michaela told them both how miserable she had been in her new school, how the other students had treated her. Both Nana and Mama were extremely mad, even with Michaela. "Why did you not tell us?" cried Nana.

"I was afraid," replied Michaela. "I wanted to show I could do well. I'm sorry I failed you."

"You didn't fail us," said Mama. "We failed you. On Monday, you will not go to that school again. I will not allow it. You are going back to your old school."

Mama did not lie. On Monday, she went to visit the principal at her new school, and then the superintendent of the district, the man in charge of all schools. Michaela didn't want her to name names, but Michaela wasn't invited to the meetings, so she really didn't know what Mama said. All she knew was that come Tuesday, she could return to her old school.

That might have been the end of it, but the following year, who should appear at Michaela's school but Ellie and Melissa! Apparently, the district had changed the bussing so that now they came to her. Michaela was more than kind and surprisingly happy to see them. Their friendship actually bloomed throughout the year.

As for Rachel, the girls informed Michaela that she had gone off the deep end. She just became more and more crazy, dropping out before the end of the year before. They never saw her afterwards, and they never called for Bloody Mary ever again!

Mijita, DO YOU UNDERSTAND THIS STORY? *Sí* IT IS VERY SAD.

The girls were mean, and I do not want you to ever act that way. No, and it is *muy importante*, very important, that you never play with the board called La Ouija. It is evil, *muy mal*. And you must not call the Bloody Maria. She, too, is *muy mala*. I do not want to lose *mi nieta*, my granddaughter. I love you, *te quiero*. Do not call into the mirror, *el espejo*, and do not look for the Bloody Mary. *Sí* she is there, but she will take you.

8

JACKPOT!

THERESA SNATCHED the roll of quarters from the change girl and hurried over to the west end of the casino, where they had her favorite machines. Without pausing to speak to the patrons she knew as the regulars, she rushed over to the slot machine on the end of the row closest to the door. Clenching her quarters wrapped in white paper with red lettering, she cracked the roll on the edge of the jackpot tray in front of the machine. It was time to play.

The Double D Casino was old-fashioned, but that gave it charm as far as Theresa was concerned. Newer gambling establishments had slot machines with a place to feed your money, and winnings were paid by a voucher, but not the Double D. This casino made you feed in your money one coin at a time and when you won, they paid one coin at a time. These slot machines didn't even have buttons you could hit. Instead, gamblers had to pull the handle every single time they prayed for luck. These charms gave the place character, and they made Theresa's experience last a little longer than newer versions. Theresa could savor the event and make the encounter more memorable.

A cacophony of noise enveloped Theresa: change dropping into the metal trays, music blaring from winning machines, and the never ending "dings" as she and the players around her dropped their coins into the slots. Despite the volume, Theresa heard none of it. She was hypnotized by the action in front of her and noticed very little else. The slot machine was her world now, at least until the quarters ran out.

Unfortunately, that didn't take long.

ON HER WAY THROUGH THE PARKING LOT, THERESA BUMPED into an old friend.

"*Hola*, Theresa. I have not seen you in a long while. *¿Cómo estás?*"

"I'm fine," Natalia replied. "Busy, but fine. How are you?"

"*Bien.* How did you do on the machines today? Are you a big winner?"

"I am sorry to say I have not had much luck in quite a while. And you?"

"No. My luck has vanished, but did you hear about Lucia?" Natalia spoke of a mutual friend. "She won big three times on one visit last month, and then won the car! *Sí*, the red convertible just inside the entryway. Can you believe it? I haven't seen her since or I would tease her. Instead, I just come and lose." Despite her bad luck, Natalia smiled.

Theresa grinned as well. Patting her friend's shoulder, she laughed and said, "I haven't seen Lucia either, but when I do, I'll have to ask her to share the luck. But for now, I really must hurry home. Bye, Natalia."

Without another word, Theresa proceeded toward her car. Though she enjoyed chatting with her friend, she didn't dare stop again. If she didn't hurry, she would be late, and that would mean trouble, big trouble.

Last year she developed a problem with the casino. She was stopping every day after work, and sometimes the time got away from her. Once, she actually forgot to pick Ricky up from school. Diego was furious when the school called, and he had to take off from work to pick him up. When she finally arrived home, she told Diego she had car trouble and that a friend from work had to jump her battery. That calmed him down.

However, when Diego found out that Theresa had spent nearly half their savings, he could not be calmed. She couldn't think of any logical explanation, so she told him the truth. Their money had gone to the slot machines. Diego looked ready to explode. He left that night and didn't return until the next morning. That was when he gave Theresa an ultimatum.

"Theresa, I love you but I cannot live with lies," Diego explained that morning. "You must promise not to lie to me again and pledge not to return to the casino. I worry because you have a problem and need to stay away from that place. If you can make me those vows, I can forgive you."

Theresa agreed to the conditions, and she meant to keep them. It was just so hard!

It wasn't all bad. She did slow down on her gambling. Now she only visited the casino once a week, on Fridays. Diego thought she was at a meeting of Gamblers Anonymous. He respected her privacy and rarely asked about the meetings, so at least she didn't have to tell more lies. As long as she was careful and avoided blowing it like last time, she figured Diego wouldn't really mind. After all, it was her money, too, and she was always mindful not to lose too much. Nobody was hurt.

Of course, life would be much better if she could just win a big jackpot. Then Diego would understand, she thought. Then he wouldn't complain if she was a little late.

"Well, I haven't won a ton of money, so I'd better step on it," she said aloud to herself. She eased the car out of the parking lot and was on her way.

Fifteen minutes later, Theresa pulled into her driveway.

Ricky, her ten-year-old son, came running out to the car.

"Did you remember, Mama? Did you remember?"

"Remember what?"

"Oh, Mama. You promised. You said you would stop and get me a new helmet so I can ride my bike. You promised!"

"Oh, *Mijito*, I'm sorry. I forgot. Please don't be angry with me. How about if we go to the store together? We can go first thing in the morning."

"Okay, Mama." Ricky walked away shaking his head. Mama was always forgetting her promises, but that didn't make it any easier. He was disappointed and sad, but he guessed he could wait one more day. He looked back at his mother. "You won't forget again tomorrow, will you Mama?"

"If I do, you can remind me. Don't worry. We'll get the darn helmet." Theresa was almost angry with him for continuing to push her. After all, she said she'd do it, didn't she?

They headed into the house together and Diego met them in the kitchen. "How was your meeting?" he asked as he bent down to kiss her cheek.

"*Bien.* It was fine." Theresa's glare told Diego she didn't appreciate his question. "I don't want to talk about it. Just leave me alone, would you?" Walking down the hall toward their bedroom, she called, "I need a little time to unwind. Just leave me alone for a while, okay?" The bedroom door slammed.

Diego looked at Ricky. "What brought that on?" he asked his son.

"She forgot to buy my helmet. I guess I made her mad when I asked about it. I'm sorry, Papa."

"It is not your fault, *Mijo*. Your mama must have had a bad day. Let's surprise her by fixing dinner. Maybe that will cheer her up."

"What do you want to fix for dinner?"

"How about leftovers?" his father replied. "There are *chiles rellenos* and *tamales* in the freezer. We could thaw them in the microwave."

"Can we have *frijoles*, too?"

"I think I can manage that. Let's get started."

SOON, THE AROMA OF THE LEFTOVERS PERMEATED THE ENTIRE house. Theresa quietly returned from their bedroom. She saw that the table was already set, and the food was hot and ready. Feeling rather foolish for her earlier outburst, she muttered something under her breath, drawing attention that she was in the room.

Diego looked up and saw her in the doorway. "*¡La cena está servida!* Dinner is served!" he announced.

Cautiously, Theresa met his eyes. "*Lo siento.* I'm sorry. I am a fool, *una tonta. Por favor perdóname.* Please forgive me. Our dinner smells wonderful."

"Well, that's because it is your leftovers. All we did was

heat them up, but we will still accept the compliment, right, Ricky?"

Ricky grinned and ran to hug his mama. "Let's eat!" he shouted.

They sat down to a lovely dinner. Everyone had a wonderful evening, and the next day Theresa bought Ricky the best helmet they could find. That weekend was nearly perfect, and the good times continued throughout the week.

EVERYTHING WAS GOING GREAT, UNTIL THE NEXT FRIDAY came to pass.

Theresa was back at the Double D Casino, right on schedule. She had actually considered skipping her visit this week, but then she became convinced that this would be her big day. She just couldn't miss it. What if she squandered her chance, and then she never got another one? No, she was going to hit the machines, at least for a while. Today just might be the day her luck changed. Just to make sure, she had placed her Rosary beads in the sweater pocket.

"Theresa, I am glad you have come today!" It was her friend, Natalia, who greeted her as she entered through the glass doors and walked quickly past the security personnel. Natalia was wiping black residue from her hands. She had obviously been inside the casino already, as the coins left their mark. "Have you heard the news? There have been many big winners today. Maybe it will be our turn, too." Natalia was flushed with excitement.

"I certainly hope so, Natalia. I'm going for change. Maybe I'll see you at the machines." Theresa fingered her beads in impatience.

"But Theresa," Natalia stopped her friend before she

could enter. "I need to tell you that our friend Lucia is missing. Her family has filed *un reporte de persona desaparecida*, a missing persons report. No one has seen her since she won the beautiful car."

"No, I had not heard," replied Theresa. She paused a moment to wonder, then waved to her friend and continued on her quest without taking any heed.

Once inside, Theresa searched for a change girl, but there were none in sight. Resigning herself to standing in line, she headed over to the booth with the bright red neon lights. It made more sense than waiting until a change person finally strolled by. She was ready!

Arriving at the change booth, Theresa fell in line behind an elderly couple who were searching for their money. The woman's purse was as big as a small suitcase. "Great. I'll be here all day," Theresa muttered to herself.

"Do you want change, *Señora?*"

Theresa looked up to see a tall dark stranger in line behind her. "Pardon me?" she inquired.

"Do you need change? I just happen to have a few rolls of quarters here with me. Would you like some?"

Theresa glanced back at the couple ahead of her. They were still fumbling in the woman's handbag.

"Well, yes, thank you. I would appreciate it if I could get some quarters from you." She handed him a twenty-dollar bill which he exchanged for two rolls. "Thank you. You are quite kind."

"*Señora,* if you do not mind, could I have one more minute of your time?"

"Well, I'm running late and I do want to get to my machine," Theresa replied. Her mind raced to think of any excuse to allow her to get to her machine. Then she hesitated. Maybe it would be best to show a little courtesy. After all, what goes around comes around, right? "What can I do for you?" she asked.

"It is not what you can do for me, *Señora,* but what I can do for you. I know a machine that is soon to pay off. May I show you?"

Theresa was skeptical. "How do you know it's about to pay off?"

"Just trust me, Señora. Come. I will show you." The stranger took Theresa by the arm and led her around the change booth. Strolling by the poker machines and the dollar slots they finally stopped in front of a Red, White, and Blue Lucky Seven machine. "Here it is, *Señora.* This is the machine you should play."

"But I usually play the Quick Hit machines on the other side," Theresa explained. "Besides, if this machine is about to pay off, why don't you play it?"

"Trust me, *Señora.* Trust me. It will make me happy to see you win."

Theresa shrugged. Well, what the heck? It certainly couldn't hurt to take his advice. Plopping herself in the seat, she sat down in front of the machine. "Well, all right. I'll give it a whirl!" She cracked the quarters and broke the roll, quickly dropping three coins into the slot, then pulled the lever. Her eyes were glued to the screen in front of her. The first wheel stopped with a clunk. Cherry. The second one followed. Cherry. Finally, the third. Cherry.

"Hey, you were right!" she said as she turned around. "I won twenty dollars!" She found herself talking to thin air. She looked around the rows of machines, but he was nowhere to be found. "Man, that was weird," she whispered. "But I might as well play on!"

She dropped another three quarters into the machine, reached up, and gave the handle a tug. The rollers in the machine flew by until the first one stopped. A Red Seven. The second one halted. A White Seven. Theresa held her breath. The third one finally quit. A Blue Seven.

"Oh my God!" Theresa screamed. She'd hit the jackpot! The lights above the row of machines started flashing and a siren went off. Everyone around her came over to see what she had won.

"She hit the big one!" she heard someone say. "How much did it pay?"

"I can't tell. How much is it, Fred?"

"Looks like she won fifteen hundred. Not bad!"

Fifteen hundred. Did he say fifteen hundred? Was that fifteen hundred dollars? Theresa couldn't believe it. Did she actually win fifteen hundred dollars?

The quarters quit flying out of the machine, so Theresa looked around.

"Don't touch the machine!" yelled a man behind her.

"They have to come and pay you the rest of your money."

"Yeah. The machine only pays out two hundred in quarters. They'll bring you cash for the rest," said the lady next to her.

Suddenly a casino security man showed up at Theresa's side. "Well, it appears we have another big winner today. You're the sixth one, lady." He smiled at Theresa as he waved to a man in a blue suit. "Over here, Joe. We've got another big winner!"

"Looks like you're right, as usual, Bob. Good job, miss. You stay put and I'll be back with your winnings in a minute or two."

Theresa didn't say a word. She was just too stunned as she sat looking at the machine, wondering if this were really a dream. Could it actually be true?

It wasn't long before Joe returned with a fist full of bills.

"Hold out your hand, miss. I'm about to pay you a lot of money." He smiled as he started to count out the hundred dollar bills. "One hundred, two hundred, three, four...." He stopped when he reached thirteen hundred. "Now, add that to the quarters in your tray and you should have fifteen hundred dollars. Not bad for a seventy-five cent investment. You must be lucky today!"

"Uhhh," Theresa stammered. "Thank you. Thank you very much."

"You're welcome, miss. Now go win some more!" Joe said. "You need to play it off."

"Excuse me? I don't understand."

"You have to put at least another quarter in and play off the jackpot. Go ahead. We all want to see you win again."

Theresa picked up three more quarters and placed them in the machine. She pulled the handle and the wheels started to spin, but this time when they stopped there was no winner.

"Well, you can't win 'em all," said Bob, the security man. He smiled at Theresa and Joe shook her hand while wishing her continued good luck. With that, they were gone, and the crowd around Theresa started to dissipate. Many people congratulated her as they passed by. She was floating on clouds and wondered if it were all a dream, but she knew it wasn't. Those hundred dollar bills were real!

Eventually, Theresa was alone with her lucky machine. She thought about playing it for a while more, but didn't have that lucky feeling. It probably wouldn't hit again.

"So I was right, *Señora*. You are a big winner."

Theresa jumped nearly a foot in the air. The handsome stranger had startled her. When she recovered, she practically shouted as she said, "Oh yes, you were right. How can I ever thank you? Do you want half of the jackpot?"

"Oh no, *Señora*. I want only for you to win. It makes me

happy to see you win. I have no need of the money. You must keep your winnings."

"Well, I don't know what to say. Thank you. Thank you very much!"

"Do not thank me, *Señora*. It is you who pulled the handle. It is you who won.

And speaking of winning, I believe I can show you another winning game, but you must hurry. Are you ready to trust me again?"

"Oh, yes. I'll trust you."

"Then follow me, quickly!"

The stranger led Theresa to the Keno area. He sat down at one of the burgundy colored chairs with the desk attached. Theresa moved to the desk beside him.

"Take this sheet and mark the numbers I say. Just put an X on them. Ready?"

Theresa nodded.

"Mark number 6. Now 66." He paused. "What is your birthday, Señora?"

"November 30th," answered Theresa.

"That is 11 and 30. Mark those numbers. Now mark a 13. That should be all. Take the paper up to the woman at the cage and give it to her with five dollars. Tell her to make sure it is for game number six hundred sixty-six. Can you remember that?"

"Game number 666. Yes, I can remember." Theresa walked up to the Keno seller and repeated her instructions. "Okay, lady," said the woman behind the desk in a complete monotone. "You want to play five numbers for five dollars. Right?"

"I guess. But it has to be game number 666," answered Theresa.

"Yeah, well that's the game coming up, so you're all set."

The woman handed Theresa her official Keno ticket and looked up to the next person in line, her expression never changing.

"Thank you," Theresa said as she turned around to find her new friend. But where was he? He had disappeared again. Searching the room with her eyes, he was nowhere to be found.

"Game closed," the Keno announcer said with the same monotone voice. Everyone looked up to watch the balls spin in the wire cage. They fell down a chute one at a time, and the announcer called off the numbers as he lit the lights on the Keno board. In no time at all, all fifteen balls were lit.

Theresa looked up at the board and checked her numbers. Yes, there was a 6 and an 11, and a 13. Her heart started to pound as she realized that 30 and 66 were there as well. She was a winner again!

Theresa ran up to the window. "I think I won!" she shouted.

The woman took her Keno sheet and scanned it with a computer pen. "Well, it looks like you're right. You are a winner. I owe you three thousand dollars."

"THREE THOUSAND DOLLARS?" Theresa clasped her hand over her mouth. She hadn't meant to shout, but it just came out. "Three thousand dollars?" she asked again, this time in a normal voice.

The woman smiled. At least it looked close to a smile. "Yep, three thousand dollars. Just hold on a second. I have to get my supervisor to verify this."

The woman called her supervisor over and the ticket was verified. Before she knew it, Theresa was holding the cash in her hand. However, this time they made her sign a form declaring the winnings for her income tax. Theresa didn't want to make a record of it, but she didn't have any choice.

"What am I going to tell Diego?" she thought as she walked away from the Keno area. "He'll find out next year when we give our taxes to the accountant. How can I keep it from him?"

Theresa was so preoccupied that she didn't even pay attention to where she was going. Suddenly, she heard the stranger's voice again.

"Another winner? I am happy for you, *Señora*."

Theresa whirled. Where was he? She heard his voice, yet he was nowhere to be seen.

"*Si, Señora*. You have done well today. Perhaps we should meet here more often."

Where was he? This was crazy. She could hear him but couldn't see him. What was going on?

"*Señora*, I can make you rich. You like to win, do you not?"

Suddenly, Theresa realized that something was very wrong. She looked up and found herself in front of the new shiny red Ford Mustang that people were trying to win with their quarters. There, in the front seat of the car, was the stranger. In the passenger seat, she saw her friend, Lucia, sitting very straight, her eyes glazed over. Lucia looked haggard with drooping eyes and pale, chalk-like skin. Theresa called to her friend but received no response, not even a flinch.

The mysterious stranger grinned at her. "*Señora*, do not be afraid. We are partners, remember? You win the money, and I gain a companion. Not a bad deal, would you not agree?" Theresa heard his voice, but his lips did not move. He just sat in the car grinning at her. She glanced at the other slot players. No one else seemed to notice him in the car. Apparently, they didn't hear his voice, either. Feeling like she was alone with him, Theresa pleaded with her friend Lucia to help her.

"Lucia! Lucia! What is going on? Help me!" When no acknowledgment came, Theresa turned instead to the stranger. "How did you get in there? No one is allowed in the car. Why did you help me? What are you after?"

"After? What am I after? Why, I am after you, *Señora.*

Just ask, and I will do anything for you."

With that, the stranger opened the door of the car. He turned toward Theresa and put one foot out. Theresa cried out, "You have a goat foot!" His second foot joined the first. "And a chicken foot!" Theresa began to back away from the machines, thinking she might faint. "You are the Devil!"

"*Si, Señora.* It is I, *El Diablo*, your *compañero*, your partner. Are you ready to win again?"

Theresa shrieked, and everyone around the slot machines turned to look at her. Someone asked if she needed help, but she just pushed her aside. No one else was aware of *El Diablo* or Lucia. Theresa shoved her hand in her pocket and retrieved her Rosary beads. As she ran toward the door, she began the Rosary, starting with the The Apostle's Creed.

"*Creo en Dios, Padre Todopoderoso, Creador del cielo y la tierra.*" It was weird that the Spanish version came to her first, but she switched to English. "I believe in God, the Father Almighty, Creator of Heaven and earth."

"*Señora*, wait. I thought you liked our arrangement. Why are you leaving?" *El Diablo* would not giving up that easily. Theresa didn't answer and was too terrified to even look back. "*Señora*, I understand. You want to go home to your family. But you won't tell them about our afternoon, will you? I think you should continue to keep the secrets from your husband. Make up another lie. It makes you a better *compañera* for me." Suddenly, as she was right in front of the exit, the stranger stood directly in her path.

Theresa fell to her knees and continued the Rosary prayers, moving smoothly through all six before contemplation of the Mysteries.

El Diablo attempted to break her concentration. "*Señora*, at least you could say good-bye. However, I will forgive you this time and allow you to leave, but I wait for you here. When will I see you? Next week? Or do you desire to win again sooner? Whenever you want, *Señora*. I will be here whenever you want." He reached out to take her hand but Theresa yanked it away, jumped up from her knees, and ran around him out the door to freedom, praying for salvation.

Once outside, Theresa stopped dead in her tracks. Every car in the parking lot was a shiny red Ford Mustang. It looked like a sea of crimson vehicles, and Theresa began to panic. Where was her car? What was going on? Finally, just when her panic began to escalate out of control, she saw her ratty old station wagon, the only blemish in the ruby rows of autos.

Theresa couldn't get to her car fast enough. Literally jumping into the wagon, she was able to start it in record time. Her tires screeched as she sped away. She knew exactly where she should go. The church and her priest were a few short miles away.

Careening into the church parking area, she nearly fainted at the wheel as her brakes squealed and cried in protest at her stomp on the pedal. There, right next to the front door, was the red Ford Mustang just sitting to the side.

El Diablo stood with his hand on the hood, just like a model in an advertising photo for the car. He was smiling, but the grin was definitely not pleasant.

Gloating. He's gloating, Theresa thought. She also

considered that she might faint. Luckily, she held on to consciousness.

"Señora," said the teasing voice of the Devil, "I think you may have forgotten something. Do you not wish to have this beautiful car? You could arrange to give it as a gift to your loving husband. He would like such a gift, would he not?"

There was no way Theresa was going to get into a debate or even a discussion at that point. Keeping her eyes on the Crucifix on the front door, she blindly rushed straight into her sanctuary where she was confident *El Diablo* could not follow.

Hurriedly, she took the blessing of the holy water, praying that it might help cleanse her soul. After making the sign of the Trinity, she sprinted into the cathedral's ecclesiastical haven, searching with her eyes for her priest, Father Michael. As she spotted him at the altar, she screamed his name and fell to her knees.

The vicar ran to her side with a questioning look on his face. "What is it my child? Why are you crying?" he asked.

"Oh, Father, I have made a terrible mistake. I need your help. *El Diablo* is waiting for me outside in the parking lot!"

"Come child. Let us go to the confessional, and you can tell me all about it from there."

Theresa followed the holy man and slipped into the vestibule when they arrived. Once there, Theresa spoke in extreme detail, starting from the very beginning, when she started hiding her gambling.

When finished, Theresa thought she would feel relief, but instead, she felt only additional fear. Could the priest actually help her, or was it too late?

Of course, the priest was sympathetic and wise. He instructed Theresa to take her illicit winnings and bring them to the donation box at the front of the cathedral. Once there, he explained that she had only one course to save herself. It was imperative that the ill-gotten funds be given to God and the Church. There was no choice, and it must be done immediately.

Without hesitation, Theresa shoved the money into the box, praying with Father Michael even after the money was out of sight. After that, finally, she felt relief, though she was still quite frightened.

"Father," inquired Theresa, "what can I do about *El Diablo?* He waits for me!"

"Child, *El Diablo* is always waiting for you. He waits for everyone to falter, and if you do, he will be quick to offer sympathy. You just have to ignore him and put your faith in God. Can you do that?"

Crossing herself, she stammered a bit from dread, but was able to utter a quiet "Yes, Father. I can remember my faith in the Deity."

When she exited the church, El Diablo was, indeed, still waiting for her, but when he tried to gain her attention, she ignored him and walked straight to her car. She had some explaining to do once she could arrive home, but she had faith she could succeed and repair the damage done to her marriage.

And she did.

You see, *Mijita?* Gambling is very bad, and so is the telling of lies. You must never do commit these sins.

Mi amiga, Theresa, has now learned this lesson. She will never return to a place of gambling. Theresa spends her time in Iglesia, in church now. *Sí*, she is a good woman, but she also has *suerte*. How you say? Oh, *Sí*, I remember. She is lucky. Her luck is not with cards or slot machines. No, she is blessed because she has a wonderful husband and family who have helped protect her. *Sí*, and she is fortunate because she escaped *El Diablo*. I never want to see you come close like she did. *Mantente alejado del casino.* Stay away from the Devil.

9

THE TLAHUELPUCHI (THE VAMPIRE WITCH)

(T'LA-H'WLL-POOCHI)

A LONG, long time ago, three girls grew up in a small village in Central Mexico. Their lives were somewhat boring up until they were teenagers. That's when Regina, Emma, and Magdalena set a course for misery and despair for their adult lives.

To tell the truth, everything actually started with Regina. As she was slightly older than the other girls, she entered puberty before her younger friends. When she did, her personality changed. The biggest indicator of that was the fact that Regina quit going to church. Emma and Magdalena stopped by her home every Sunday to walk with her, just as they did for practically all their lives, but Regina changed the ritual by saying she wasn't really "into" church anymore, and they should go on without her.

This routine lasted for three or four months. Then one Saturday, Regina brought up the topic about worship services to her friends. "You know," she said, "you don't have to go to church tomorrow."

"Why not?" asked Emma, the youngest of the three. "Because no one can make you go," was Regina's reply.

"You haven't heard my mother," answered Magdalena. "Same here," chimed in Emma.

"Really?" Regina rolled her eyes. "My mom was the same with me, but I told her I just don't believe in God anymore."

Both of the others gasped in shock but continued on their way to the park, a favorite hang-out. Neither Emma nor Magdalena wanted to discuss the issue, so their trek was in silence, and the subject did not come up again throughout the day.

———

THE NEXT DAY, AFTER SERVICES, THE GIRLS WENT DIRECTLY to Regina's house. It was time for an inquisition. What was going on?

Regina greeted her friends at her front door, as if expecting them. Before even one question could be uttered, she began to explain. "Don't nag at me," Regina started. "I am just tired of going to church every Sunday. Seriously, we only have two days on the weekend to enjoy ourselves. Why waste half of that on worshiping God when I am not even sure the whole concept isn't a fraud."

Neither of the other girls could think fast enough to respond, so Regina just kept talking. "Let's just forget about it, okay? Come on in. I made *sopapillas* while you two were wasting your time. Want some?"

No one in her right mind would pass up fresh, hot *sopapillas*, with the aroma permeating the house, so the girls hurried off to Regina's kitchen and began eating the fabulous pastries. Pausing only to sprinkle powdered sugar or spoon honey on their treat, each girl devoured three before she knew it.

"Oh my God," said Magdalena, patting her stomach in satisfaction. "I am so full I could burst."

Both Regina and Emma answered in unison, "Me, too!" and all three erupted into laughter. Soon, they were off on their usual walk to the park to discuss school and boys and everything in the world except the church.

This pattern became routine, except that Regina would prepare different foods for the other girls every week. It came to the point when Emma and Magdalena could hardly wait for services to end just so they could get out of there and make it to the delightful indulgence they knew awaited them.

It was only about three months later when Magdalena surprised Emma by telling her that she, too, would be skipping church. She wanted to spend the time cooking with Regina. Besides, she also was not sure of her religious convictions anymore.

Emma had to walk to services by herself and was not happy about it. That's why it really wasn't much of a surprise to Regina and Magdalena when Emma announced she would join them. At first, Emma only skipped Mass every other week, but it didn't take long for baking and cooking to take the place of God. All three girls became superb chefs.

Word spread of these three young women and their wonderful abilities. Soon, they were whipping up a scrumptious offering for everyone as they left the church. No one seemed to question their lack of attendance, because the social hour with food became a tradition. It seemed that everyone in the village was better off with the girls avoiding the rituals of Sunday sacraments. Before long, people began to split their donations between the girls and the religious center of the community. Rachel was especially thrilled by that.

Then, it happened. Another young woman, just three

years older than the "Happy Hour Hostesses" (as they called themselves), married. All three of the cooks knew this young woman quite well from school, so they were invited to the ceremony. Regina answered for them all by saying they couldn't attend the ceremony in the church but would be happy to prepare the reception feast. Emma and Magdalena were a little disappointed, because a wedding was great cause for celebration, but in the end, they figured the real party was afterwards, so preparing the food ahead of time would mean they could truly participate in the *recepción de la boda*, the wedding reception.

The fiesta was a success, and a new business was the result. Anytime there was a celebration in the village, the three girls were paid to provide the culinary delights. After many marriages, birthdays, *quinceañeras*, and even funerals, people actually forgot that the girls didn't attend church. In fact, many others began to join in with food preparation, ignoring their religious duties to prepare for gatherings held after services.

Until, that is, the *Tlahuelpuchi* became apparent. This creature lives with a human family and can "shift shapes" to become a luminous mist as well as a gigantic bird, such as a turkey or raven. These evil creatures must feed on the blood of humans once a month to stay alive. Though they prefer infants, the *Tlahuelpuchi* will feast on the lives of others, too. They live with their human family who keep their secret, because to inform anyone of the existence would bring horrible consequences for the rest of the family members.

Within this small village, Rachel, Emma, and Magdalena saw their older friends lose their babies to the witch over and over again. It was heartbreaking. The young mothers would put their babies down for the night only to return the next morning to find these precious infants dead in their cribs.

When people came to check on the adolescents' families, they noticed that scratch marks had appeared outside the doors and windows of the home. It was common to leave windows open due to the stifling heat, but that changed after the *Tlahuelpuchi* began to strike. The people of the village were fearful and kept their windows closed. However, since the *Tlahuelpuchi* could change into a mist and come in through closed doors, everyone still was anxious. The mist put everyone in the home to sleep, and the vampire witch could easily take any member of the family.

Mothers, in particular, were frantic as they feared for the lives of their babies and young children. Almost all of them returned to the church and some even began attending multiple masses during the week. The after-service gatherings took place in the churchyard, where villagers were much more at ease.

The business side of cooking also slowed down, and soon the three girls who started the tradition of meeting after church began to drift apart. The final straw came when Emma announced that she was engaged to Jesús Rivera, a boy just a few years older than her. Emma thought it would be an occasion for great celebration between the friends, and though Magdalena was happy, Rachel seemed angry with jealousy and very displeased.

As her wedding day approached, Emma asked both Regina and Magdalena to be her maids of honor, but only the latter accepted. Regina informed her friends that she would be unable to attend the church wedding, but she would be happy to prepare the food for after. She didn't appear all that happy to Emma, but Emma wouldn't let that spoil her day.

Six months later, Magdalena made the same announcement for herself and Mateo. They were to be married in the church, and again Regina refused to attend, though she didn't seem so angry this time. Emma served as Matron of Honor, and, once more, it was a wonderful celebration for the entire village. Of course, the wedding feast once again was prepared by Regina, and all seemed well.

Everything, that is, except the dreadful deaths of infants and children. These heartbreaking, horrific passings were so prevalent that the local undertaker prepared death certificates with the cause of death listed as *chupado por la bruja*, or "blood sucked by the witch."

Magdalena and Mateo were blessed with the birth of a son only one year later. Santiago was a beautiful baby and brought much joy to the family. That elation was marred only by the panic that beset all young mothers in fear of the *Tlahuelpuchi*. Luckily, no scratches were seen at her door, and after the first year, Magdalena relaxed, a least a little.

Emma was an honorary aunt to the young boy. Weekly visits from *Tía* Emma were a constant source of joy for both Magdalena and the sweet child. One time, Emma brought Regina along to meet the baby, who at that point was over two years old. The atmosphere of that visit seemed strained, and the normally outgoing youngster appeared to be leery of this new "aunt." However, as time elapsed, Santiago came to enjoy time with Regina, and she was even able to take him for outings to give his mother a much needed break every so often.

One Sunday, Emma saw Regina and Santiago at the park. She was going to stop and say hello, but Regina was in a very intense conversation with the boy. When Emma started toward them, Regina took Santiago by the arm and led him in the opposite direction. Emma, somewhat offended, decided not to dwell on this rudeness, but she always wondered just what Regina was saying to the child. It was unfortunate that she never asked.

Then, a few years later, Emma came to be pregnant, and she, just like the other young mothers of the village, became petrified thinking about her unborn baby being used as food for the *Tlahuelpuchi*. Before the child was even born, she insisted that Jesús seal all the windows and doors with materials to stop the draft and repel any air from entering their home. Jesús protested, but he could also see Emma's panic, so he did as she asked.

Once little Juan José was born, Emma refused to allow him to sleep in a separate room. It wasn't until the baby was two years old that Jesús won the battle and the toddler began to sleep in his own room across the hall. Many a night Emma sat in her rocking chair in the nursery just watching her young son doze. She kept a small fire in the torch used for light just so she could see her little one as he slept. Sometimes, the nervous young mother had as many as four torches lit in his room. "It will keep him safe," she told Jesús.

Though Emma never completely gave up her ritual of sitting with her baby son every night, she did eventually limit her time there to the telling of two or three bedtime stories and then joining her husband in their bed. The only stipulation made by the young boy was that she had to leave a light, as he was deathly afraid of the dark. This was easily remedied by the four small candles Emma lit for him every night, burning them throughout the night to calm her frightened son.

One Sunday, Magdalena and Santiago came to visit and brought Regina with them. Though the precious baby was less than a year old, Juan José had a simply dreadful reaction when Regina went to pick him up and hold him. The brought forth from such a tiny person sounded more like those of a full-grown adult. There was no way that child was going to be held by *Tía* Regina. He was a perfect angel for Magdalena, and even young Santiago could cuddle the baby without incident, but every time Regina came near him, the babe let out yet another blood- curdling howl. Emma was embarrassed, but nothing could be done to change her young son's attitude toward Regina.

As little Juan José grew, his feelings for Regina never changed. When he was old enough to talk, he told his mama that *Tía* Regina made him scared. There was no way he was going to be calm around her, so eventually, Regina stopped trying to visit, and Emma actually was happier that way, as she felt uneasy herself when Regina came near her beautiful, healthy young son.

Sadly, poor little Juan José became very ill shortly after his fourth birthday. The hospital in Santa Paula became his home soon after he turned five. Emma had to move closer to the facility to be near her young son, accepting an invitation to stay with nearby relatives, and Jesús stayed behind to continue his employment to help pay for the hospital bills, which became quite extensive.

As weeks and months passed, it became apparent that the little boy would not make it to see his sixth birthday, so Jesús came to join his wife. Emma and Jesús spent every day and night at the hospital with Juan José, but the toll of the stress began to show on Emma. She became increasingly gaunt and eventually fell ill herself. Jesús finally had to put his foot down and insist that she spend each night at the relatives' home, while he stood guard with their young son. Emma resisted, but she was much too weak to continue her protests and gave up, staying away in hopes of increasing her stamina.

One night in November, a cousin from the home where the parents were staying came to inform Jesús that Emma's health was declining at a furious rate. Torn between his promise to stay with their son and dismay for his wife, Jesús decided to sit with the boy until midnight and then go to the home to check on his wife. When he left, he was very careful to leave a candle for light for his sickly son. Emma would never forgive him if he forgot.

Jesús quietly slipped away at midnight and made his way to his wife's bedside, never actually sleeping but nodding off often. The stress and worry were affecting him as well.

IN THE MORNING, JESÚS WENT IMMEDIATELY TO THE HOSPITAL even before his sickly wife had awakened. As he approached, he saw scratch marks outside the window leading to Juan José's hospital room. In fact, there were scratch marks all around the windows and doors to every room, though the indentations were much more pronounced at his son's window. Alarmed, Jesús rushed inside to check on his son.

Juan José was nowhere to be found. After notifying the entire hospital staff, Jesús began to check every room, every space. Nurses and doctors soon joined in, and the hunt soon went beyond the hospital.

Outside, just next door to the hospital, was the *Panteón de Belén*, the well-known Cemetery of Santa Paula. Suddenly, Jesús found his stomach filled with a forlorn knot, a sign so to speak. He rushed to the cemetery, calling his son's name. No response was heard, but it didn't take long before he found the little one's dead body. Jesús let out a shriek that could be heard for miles. He immediately scooped the boy's body into his arms, and even though he knew Juan José was gone, he frantically ran to the hospital and demanded that someone help the poor boy. Sadly, there was nothing to be done.

The prospect of giving Emma the news of their son's

death was enough to make Jesús want to run away, but he knew he must be the one to break the news. Emma reacted as any mother would do, dropping to her knees and wailing a mournful cry that tore at everyone's heart. When Jesús told her that he had been with her the night before and did not stay for the entire night with their son, Jesús was sure Emma would never forgive him, but her reaction was quite different. She told her husband there would be no blame because laying fault would just make more grief.

However, Emma expressed a concern that worried Jesús. Emma kept saying, "How can we put my baby into the ground for his funeral? He is afraid of the dark!" Though Jesús tried to console her and show her the illogical nature of this fear, Emma would not give up. Instead, she cried all day and night.

WHEN THE DAY OF THE FUNERAL FINALLY CAME, JESÚS HOPED that Emma would be comforted. It was true that she seemed calmer, but Jesús knew her fear and sorrow were still imminent. He hoped that by saying a final good-bye to their son, he and Emma might be able to return to a life of somewhat normality.

Juan José was buried in the *Panteón de Belén* on a cold, wet November morning. Jesús was anxious to return to their own village, even if it was only a short distance away. Emma, on the other hand, wanted to stay and have a few more opportunities to visit the grave of her son. Jesús was wise to relent, as he knew that if they returned to their home before Emma was ready, it would be to his detriment.

THE NEXT MORNING, JESÚS AND EMMA RETURNED TO THE desolate cemetery to say prayers for their son. Their shock when they saw the scene that awaited them was indescribable. Whereas yesterday, they saw a finished gravesite with a beautiful headstone, today the grave had been excavated, and the casket lay above the hollow cavity that was their son's final resting place. Emma was still not well, and Jesús worried that this shock could send her health spiraling, so he returned her to the relatives where they'd been staying, assuring her that he would make it his mission to correct the situation by speaking to the cemetery staff.

Jesús did as promised. The workers at the *Panteón* were as shocked as he, but promised to rectify the desecration immediately, assuring the grieving father that all would be well the next day.

Being somewhat leery of subjecting his wife to another shock, Jesús went to visit the grave again the next morning. Thank God he had not escorted Emma that morning, as the casket lay outside the grave once again. Furious, Jesús confronted the cemetery staff and demanded to know why his son's coffin had not been returned to the grave as he had demanded. Shocked, the workers swore they had, indeed, reburied the coffin and had no explanation for why it was once again above ground. Of course, they promised once again to remedy this horrible state of affairs. They set to work immediately, and Jesús stood guard to make sure the task was accomplished.

Deciding he was too overcome with grief and shock, Jesús waited until the next day to escort Emma to the *Panteón* to pray for their son. Much to their disbelief, the casket was once more sitting above ground, and yet again, Jesús had to escort his wife back to the relations with whom they stayed. That time, Jesús told everyone what had been happening. It was a miserable discussion, and no one could offer any suggestions.

The situation with the coffin and gravesite continued for eight more days, when suddenly Emma had an idea. "My baby is afraid of the dark! He wants his resting place to be up and out of the earth! We forgot to give him light!"

Jesús and the cemetery staff were not as sure as Emma, but they were willing to give anything a try, so they constructed pylons to hold a raised concrete mausoleum. On each corner a stone mason etched a torch to offer never-ending light for the boy. The casket was then placed in its new home above ground.

The tension in the air the following day was like a sticky substance that engulfed everyone who tried to find relief for this boy and his parents. Jesús and Emma could barely make the short journey to the cemetery. Nerves were at the breaking point as they all entered the *casa de todos los muertos*, the cemetery. As they approached the gravesite of little Juan José, the group let out a spontaneous and synchronized gasp. The coffin was undisturbed. Everyone knelt and immediately said a prayer of thanks.

After staying for a few more days of undisturbed bliss, Jesús and Emma finally felt they could leave their baby in his grave and return to their own village. After all, the *Panteón de Belén* was only a day's walk from their home. Visiting the grave would not be too much of a burden.

Within an hour of their return, Emma was in a rush to see her friend, Magdalena. Somehow, Emma simply felt that by sharing her devastating burden with her *amiga*, the pain and sorrow might ease, at least *un poquito*, a little bit.

Unfortunately, Magdalena had her own sorrow with which to contend. Her son, just four years older that Emma's Juan José, was very ill and his mother feared for his life, just as Emma had done. Magdalena had found scratches, too, at her doors and windows. The *Tlahuelpuchi* was after her Santiago; she was sure of it.

Emma found that the best cure for her own sadness was to try to help her friend, so she suggested they both go to Regina's house and then the three of them go to the church to pray. Magdalena refused, saying that she had already tried to talk to their friend and had been shunned. Besides, Magdalena had not attended services in years, and she feared she was no longer welcome.

After Emma confessed that she, too, had not been to the sanctuary in an extended amounted of time, Magdalena finally relented, and the two of them shuffled rather sheepishly to the house of worship. Once there, the priest acted like they had never been away. He knelt with them in prayer for a long, extensive petition to God, pleading for the soul of Juan José and the health of Santiago. Neither mother minded the length of the appeal or the time it took. They simply pleaded with God to care for their sons, in heaven and on earth.

As the women were leaving the house of worship, the priest asked them to wait in the rectory for just a few moments. He left, but returned quickly with two small medallions in his grasp. For Emma, he presented a medal to be worn around her neck depicting Saint Gertrude, patron saint of the recently deceased. Magdalena received a small statue of Saint Peregrine. The priest informed her that he had a vision showing that her son, Santiago, was dying of cancer.

He suggested that Magdalena give the statue to her son and then both she and her son should offer prayers. The women were heartened by the words of the cleric.

Arriving back at Magdalena's home, Emma kissed her friend and left her to minister to Santiago. The eager mother rushed to her son's room only to find him in more pain than she had ever seen. Quickly thrusting the statue into his grasp, Magdalena started praying aloud, pausing only to ask her son to pray with her. Instead, the boy flung the statue across the room.

"Why should I pray now?" he asked. "You never took me to church or taught me the ways of God. I don't believe in such nonsense. Keep that stupid statue away from me!"

At that exact moment, Magdalena felt the full weight of the foolishness of her youth. She had turned her back on God and neglected her duties to teach her son the way of goodness and faith. Breaking into sobbing tears, she beseeched her son to forgive her and begged God to forgive him. Santiago screamed at her to go away.

Magdalena was crushed. The son she loved with all her heart had sent her away after crushing the small statue of the saint. What was she to do? She ran the entire way back to the church, where she prayed for three straight hours.

Sadly, her prayers went unanswered. Upon returning to her home, she found her precious son in more pain than ever. The doctor of her village arrived but said he had nothing to offer. He suggested that the parents, Magdalena and Mateo, take their ailing son to the hospital in Santa Paula. Perhaps the doctors there could help.

Magdalena knew that Emma had been at that same hospital with Juan José, so her first thought was to run to her friend. After desperate tears were shed, Emma agreed to accompany Magdalena to Santa Paula, because Mateo could not miss work. Jesús wasn't thrilled, but he knew the grief of mothers all too well, so it was with his blessing that Emma set out with Magdalena and Santiago on the trip to the hospital.

After leaving their village at dawn, the women and sick

child arrived in the late afternoon. Santiago slept for the entire trip. His mother was glad for that, as she didn't want him to rant or rave in front of Emma. It was better if no one else knew of his blasphemy.

Once admitted to the hospital, however, everyone became all too aware of Santiago's lack of faith. He cried out often in pain but just as often shouted insults to God. The greater his pain, the louder his foul language. Magdalena was humiliated but kept praying at his bedside nonetheless. Emma was usually at her side echoing her pleas to God.

In the evenings, Emma insisted that her friend leave the hospital to stay with the same relatives with whom Emma had lived while she was in Santa Paula. Magdalena did not want to leave Santiago's side, but his constant insults and belittling were just too much. Emma had to protect her friend from the abuse, even if the boy was sick. Emma feared that her friend would break down if she didn't have time away.

After only a week, Emma and Magdalena returned to the hospital one morning to a curious sight. Scratches on the window outside Santiago's room were quite evident, and they saw barefoot child tracks in the dirt leading to the cemetery. Also found there were extremely large bird markings like none they had ever seen before. Both women entered the hospital screaming in search of Santiago, but he was nowhere to be found. Everyone headed to the *Panteón de Belén*.

They found a gut-wrenching scene when they arrived. Santiago hung from the large tree in the middle of the sanctuary with a sheet wrapped around his neck. The poor boy was swaying in the breeze but no life came from his eyes. He was gone, dead to this world.

Magdalena was so overcome that she had to be hospitalized. Emma made the trip back to their village by herself. It was the only way to inform Mateo, and when she did, Santiago's father turned completely white. Not waiting for morning, Mateo instead started sprinting toward the hospital, even though it was half a day away or more, depending on his pace.

Emma went to Jesús and convinced him to accompany her back to Santa Paula the next morning. She couldn't stand the thought of her friend's grief and the misery Emma knew only too well. Their friends were in need, so they really had no choice. That was what friends did for one each other.

After Santiago's funeral, there was no mysterious displacement of his coffin, thankfully. It seemed like the poor boy would be able to rest in peace. On the other hand, Emma fretted about her friend. Magdalena seemed so fragile, like a porcelain doll, ready to crack if dropped.

The night after the funeral, Magdalena asked Emma to come with her to the cemetery. She wanted to pray for both of their sons. Emma was only too glad to accept. Mateo and Jesús had been locked in secret discussions, and she would just as soon get away.

Once at the *Panteón*, the women sat on a concrete bench and began their litanies for their sons. They had recited only a couple when, all of a sudden, Magdalena cried out. "Look! Oh my God, Emma! Do you see what I see?"

Unfortunately, Emma did see, and it was terrifying. Across the courtyard where the large tree sat, both women could see the shadow of a small boy swinging from the branches. Magdalena dashed toward the shadow. Emma rushed just as quickly to find their husbands.

When Emma and the men returned, the silhouette was still visible, and once they found Magdalena, all four adults clung to each other. This wasn't just chilling; it was petrifying for each of them. Thank God the men were able to lead their wives away. Everyone had tears streaming down their faces.

The next night, both couples asked hospital staff and villagers alike to stay with them for prayers after sunset. A group of nearly twenty people agreed, and that same cluster of well-wishers witnessed exactly what the parents had seen the evening before. Though extremely sympathetic, the assembly dispersed in record time. Everyone had seen the shadow and each person was terrified beyond words.

After a week or so, the phantom silhouette stopped its nightly visits. That was a blessing, thought Emma, because had it gone on, her friend, Magdalena, would have lost her mind. Maybe they all would have done the same.

The secret conversations between Mateo and Jesús continued even after the group returned to their homes. Magdalena was in no shape to notice, but Emma was well aware. She asked her husband for details. Why were they talking in such a clandestine manner?

Jesús had no answers for Emma and simply asked her to trust him. Emma figured she didn't have much choice, so she let it go.

Mateo and Jesús continued their nightly meetings. They kept the topic a secret, but in truth, they discussed the *Tlahuelpuchi*. Both men were convinced that they knew the identity of the witch. Determined to rid their village of this malevolent and immoral creature, they first had to design a plan with the least amount of danger. Everyone knew that if someone tried to kill the *Tlahuelpuchi* and failed, that person was doomed, as were his accomplices. Even his family members could suffer. It was more than important that they plan their attack; it was essential. Failure was not an option.

One month after Santiago's death, Mateo and Jesús met in the village square at twilight with guns and clubs. They made their way silently through the village. Suddenly, a huge raven appeared before them, making shrill noises. Each man swore it gave them a look known as the "evil eye." Steadying their firearms, both men shot at the creature, missing its body but destroying one of its legs. The raven shrieked and somehow flew away.

The next day, Mateo and Jesús insisted that their wives accompany them to visit their friend Regina. When they reached her home, her mother came to the door and explained that Regina would not be available. She had been involved in a horrible accident the night before and had lost her right leg. Unfortunately, Regina died before a doctor could be summoned.

Emma and Magdalena let out a cry and took Regina's mother into their arms. It did, however, seem that the mother was not as bereaved as they had imagined she would be. Jesús and Mateo exchanged a strange glance and said nothing.

The *Tlahuelpuchi* was not heard from again, at least in that village. Hopefully, she would never be spotted anywhere.

MIJO, MIJA, DO YOU NOT SEE HOW THIS STORY IS MUY Importante? I have proof that this is true. My *bisabuela*, my great-grandmother, lost her first child to the *Tlahuelpuchi*. *Sí*, I have the death certificate that says so. This story, it teaches us all a lesson, *una lección*. We must never give up our faith in God. No, our worship every Sunday helps to protect everyone in *la familia*. *Sí*, it is true we have not heard of the *Tlahuelpuchi* in a long while, but that does not mean she cannot come again. Be careful, *mis nietos*. Say your prayers and go to church. Never let the evil *bruja*, the Vampire Witch, enter your lives.

10

EL HOMBRE CABRA DE LA MONTAÑA "A" (THE GOAT MAN OF "A" MOUNTAIN)

HE ROLLED over and felt his stomach lurch. Trying to keep from throwing up, he swayed and clutched his head and then fumbled in his coat pocket to retrieve his last bottle of Everclear, a vile-tasting clear alcohol. Strong stuff, but he needed it. Anyone with a life as screwed up as his had to stay drunk. It was a rule.

He got up and moved along the railroad track. How did he get here? Oh yeah, the freight train. He remembered hopping on the moving cars back in Albuquerque. Now he was stuck here in Tucson. *Well, this certainly is some vacation spot*, he thought. *It must be 115 degrees in the shade, if you could find any shade.* The heat made him feel sicker than ever. Or maybe it was the Everclear.

What was he doing wearing a coat in this heat? He tugged and clutched at his sleeves until he was free of his red blazer, then wadded it into a ball to use as a pillow. Exhausted, he lay down on the track and peered up at the mountain to the west. It had a huge white "A" on the side. *How quaint,* he thought. *That must be "A" Mountain. Just one more thrill in this godforsaken place.*

The bottle of Everclear knocked his tooth as he raised it to his lips. *Just let me forget this place,* he thought. *Let me forget my life. Let me forget everything.* Within minutes he had passed out, drunk and unconscious. Night came quickly.

HE NEVER HEARD THE TRAIN. THE CONDUCTOR SAW HIM AT the last minute and blew his whistle like a scream in the night, but it didn't matter. It was too late.

Of course, he woke at the last split second. He didn't even have time to form a thought. The train was just there, and then his legs were not. They were cut off just below the hips. Funny thing was, there wasn't much blood. It was like they were seared off. Not much pain, either. Weird.

Then he started to think. Ten seconds ago, he was a man. Now, he was a...what? He finally was able to throw up the liquor and bile of his three-day binge.

Scanning the area around the train yard, he wiped vomit from his chin. His eyes caught the gleam of the "A" on the mountain. For some reason, he felt drawn to that "A" and made up his mind right there and then. *If I'm going to die*, he thought, *I want to die up there.*

He paused only long enough to struggle into his coat. Though it took all of his strength, he began to pull himself off the tracks and toward the mountain. Once his hands became raw from the gravel, he used his elbows. That helped some, because they were protected by the sleeves of his blazer. *Good old coat*, he thought. *Those other hoboes made fun of it because it was such a bright red.* He didn't mind. In fact, he was glad he was going to die in that coat. It made him look special.

The torturous quest took hours. He had to stop often to

quell the queasiness in his gut. Eventually, he reached the east bank of the Santa Cruz River (actually, a huge wash) and found himself rolling down its steep edge. Surprisingly, that helped, because when he got to the bottom, he found it easier to just keep rolling across the sandy floor. When he finally crossed the wash, it nearly killed him to climb the other bank. Still, he never gave up. He was headed to the "A" and was determined to make it before he died.

Once he climbed the bank, he looked up and found himself at the foot of the mountain. Keeping his eyes focused on his goal, he clawed and crawled up the side of the hill. It was well after midnight when he finally reached his destination. Tears of joy mixed with his sorrow as he laid his head upon the white stones. He was ready to die.

But wait. What was that? There was a glow from the ground below him. He was mesmerized as he watched a shadowy figure appear.

"I have brought you a gift, my son," said the apparition. "It is a goat."

"What? You brought me a goat? I don't understand." "I will make you immortal. I will make you my son." "Please, leave me alone. I don't want your pity."

"I do not pity you. I admire you. I will make you mine." The figure then produced a huge blade and slaughtered the goat without another word. The man sat, horrified, as goat blood splattered and ran down his body. Then the figure took the back legs of the goat and severed them from the mutilated corpse. "These are for you." The man screamed but could not move away. The figure crouched above him and began to sew the goat legs onto the stumps left by the train.

"Do not struggle!" commanded the figure.

The man covered his face and wept. When the

transformation was complete, he looked up. "What have you done to me?"

"Oh, do not thank me. Your happiness is thanks enough."

The man glared at the strange figure and then he started to laugh. It was a howling laugh that pierced the night like thunder, and his eyes flashed like lightning. Was it gratitude reflected there? Hatred? Sorrow? Worship? No, it was simply insanity. The goat man was now completely and utterly insane.

"Come on, Maria," pleaded Hector. "We've been dating for over three weeks. It's time for a little fun."

"Hector, you know I like you. I just don't feel comfortable with too much necking and kissing."

"How do you know? You haven't even let me try! Come on, Maria, it's time for something more. You can't expect me to wait forever. I would hate to have to break up just because you were too immature to get closer."

"I'm not immature!"

"Well, do you think all of the other girls just sit and hold hands with their boyfriends? No, they don't, because they are becoming women. How about you, Maria? Are you ready to grow up a little?"

"I'm frightened, Hector."

Hector sighed, and moved his arm behind the car seat and over Maria's shoulder. "I understand, my sweet. I have an idea. Let's just drive up to "A" Mountain and park. We can look at the city lights and just take things easy. What do you think?"

"Okay. I would like that." "We'll be there in no time."

Hector eased his Corvair around the winding road that led

to the lookout at "A" Mountain. He could hardly contain his excitement, and he had to keep reminding himself to take the turns with caution. Yes, he was in a hurry to get parked and see where this night would lead, but there was no use in being careless. He'd waited three weeks. He could wait another five minutes.

When at last they had reached the base of the white stone "A," Hector slid the car into an open space behind a dark green Ford pick-up. A baby blue Volkswagen Beetle was parked farther up the road. He turned to face Maria. "See? This isn't so bad, is it?"

"Actually, I have to admit that it really is quite breathtaking. Thanks for bringing me here, Hector."

Hector didn't answer. Instead he took her face in his hands and leaned forward to kiss her. At first, she stayed quite stiff, but with a little persistence, Hector persuaded her to relax in his embrace. *All right*, he thought. *Now it's time to make my move.*

He slid his hand down Maria's back. He left it there for a second and then started to move it to the front. *Almost there*, he thought.

"Hector! What's that?" Maria screamed.

"What? Good grief, Maria. What did you scream for? I was just beginning to feel close to you."

"I'm sorry. I thought I saw something outside your window. It scared me."

"What was it?"

"I thought I saw a man in a red coat. He was looking at us."

"Come on, Maria. This is Arizona, what would anybody be doing out here in a coat?"

"I guess it just worries me to be up here."

"Well, come here and let me put your worries to rest."

Hector reached for her neck and started to nibble at her earlobe. Slowly, but surely, he felt her relax.

"You are so beautiful, Maria. I love your hair." He kissed her cheek. "And your eyes." He kissed her other cheek. "And your full, sweet lips." He brushed her lips with his own and then lingered for a longer kiss.

"Hector! There he is again! He's watching us!" This time Maria pushed him away and tried to force him to look out of his driver's side window.

"Stop it, Maria! There is nothing there. If you don't want me to kiss you, just say so. You don't have to play these stupid games!"

"Hector, I am not playing!" Maria shouted. "Just look!

Look out your window!" She was nearly hysterical.

"Fine, I'll look, and then I'm taking you ho…" Hector turned his face towards the window. What he saw made him jump. He was looking into the eyes of a crazy man in a red coat.

"What do you want?" Hector shouted through the closed window. "Get away from here! Leave us alone!"

The face grinned at Hector, and then started tap, tap, tapping on the window pane.

"What do you want?" Hector shouted again.

The man raised his arm and pointed at Maria. Then he jumped on top of the hood of the car.

That's when they saw he had goat legs. Maria screamed, and Hector started searching for his keys. The Goat Man had a hideous grin, and blood from some sort of feast drooled down his chin. Before Hector knew what was happening, the Goat Man turned around. He then raised his legs and bucked like a goat. The impact nearly shattered the front window.

"Get us out of here!" cried Maria. Hector fumbled with the keys.

"God, he's going to kick again!" Maria's eyes looked like they were going to bulge out of her head. "Watch out." She covered her face with her arms.

The Goat Man kicked, and the window imploded all over Hector and Maria. Hector's face was covered with tiny cuts from the glass. Still, he continued to wrestle with the keys in the ignition. Thankfully, they finally fit and the engine turned over. Hector threw the car into gear and revved the engine. Just as the tires quit spinning and began to make traction, Hector felt the hand of the Goat Man on his shoulder as it reached past him and grabbed Maria.

"Hey, what's going on back there?" Someone from the Ford pickup shouted.

The Goat Man looked up. It was all the distraction Hector needed. He hit the gas, released the clutch, and turned the wheel. The motion tumbled the Goat Man from the hood and onto the ground. They sped away.

THE HEADLINES IN THE PAPER THE NEXT DAY TOLD A gruesome story. A young girl had gone to "A" Mountain with her boyfriend. Sometime in the evening she vanished from his Volkswagen Beetle. The boy was found beside the road, completely incoherent. He kept mumbling something about a half-man, half-goat and a red coat. The police sent him to a sanitarium. They never found the girl.

DO YOU UNDERSTAND NOW WHY I SAY NEVER GO TO THE "A" Mountain after dark, *Mijita*? Do you see what could happen? *Mi hermana*, my sister Maria, she learned her lesson. *Sí*. She never went back and I never went either. No! You must remember this. I do not want to wake up one day and read about you in the *periódico*. You must stay away from places like "A" Mountain, *Mija. Mantente alejado del hombre cabra.* Stay away from the Goat Man.

11

NO JUEGUE CARTAS DESPUÉS DE LA MEDIANOCHE (DON'T PLAY CARDS AFTER MIDNIGHT)

THE JOKER'S WILD

"*¡MIJITAS! ¡ Mijitos!* I am going up to bed now. You need to settle down soon," cried Nana as she rose from her chair. Nana was baby sitting her grandchildren that night while her children were out of town. "I am an old woman and cannot stay up as late as you."

"Okay, Nana," replied Manny as he came in from the kitchen. "We're just playing Crazy 8s. We'll go to bed soon." He winked at his cousins like a conspirator. Felix had to muffle his laugh.

"All right, Manuel, but see that you mind the time. Remember, you must not play cards after midnight. Do not forget."

"Don't worry, Nana. We remember." He rolled his eyes, but no one else commented.

Nana headed upstairs to her room, as Manny returned to his sister and cousins in the kitchen.

"Nana says to remember not to play cards after midnight!" Manny repeated, as he strolled across the room.

Anna, Manny's little sister, and his cousins, Raul, Felix,

and Marguerite, sat around the Formica table. A deck of cards lay spread across the shining surface.

Marguerite rose from her green vinyl chair and walked over to the refrigerator. "Don't make fun of Nana. You know she takes those old tales seriously." She started rummaging through the icebox in search of leftovers from dinner.

"Hey, bring me a *tortilla*, would you, Marguerite?" "Sure, Anna. Anybody else?"

"Are there any *tostadas* left?" asked Felix. "I'm starving." "Felix, you already ate three at dinner. They're all gone." "That's okay. I'll just have some chips."

"You know, Papa says Nana is right about the cards," said Raul with a mischievous grin.

"What do you mean?" questioned Anna.

"Papa told me a story about something bad that happened to him when he played poker late at night."

"What story?" Anna looked worried.

'"Well, it goes like this," and Raul began the tale.

———

BEN WAS OUT LATE. HE KNEW HE HAD PROMISED HIS WIFE, Christina, that he would be home early, but what could he to do? Julio, one of Ben's best friends, was hosting their weekly poker game, and Ben was winning big. It would be rude, just plain ill-mannered, to leave now. No one would forgive him for leaving before they had a chance to win their money back. Besides, it was warm in there with the rugged fire blazing in the fireplace. Ben was in no hurry to go out in the cold.

Glancing around the table, Ben saw smiles on everyone's face. Besides Julio, there were Roberto and Sal. Art hadn't shown up tonight, but everyone was still enjoying their Boys' Night Out, even if they were hardly boys.

"Whose deal?" asked Julio as he snapped the top off his beer. "I am ready to start winning!"

"It is Ben's turn," replied Roberto. "It is also his turn to lose!"

All of the friends laughed. They liked to tease Ben, because he could take it and laugh right back.

"Come on, guys. I can't help it that I can do nothing but win tonight. Perhaps if you were better card players I might lose a hand or two."

"Just deal the cards," laughed Salvador. "What is the ante?" He reached across the table for another cold one.

"One dollar," replied Ben. "It is time for me to win again!"

"So much for nickel ante," grumbled Roberto. Everyone laughed as they threw their money into the middle of the small, wooden table. Despite the sneers, "I'm in!" was chorused around the room.

"I wonder why Arturo didn't show up tonight," pondered Julio as he arranged the cards in his hand.

"Oh, he's busy with that new wife of his," teased Sal. "There is no time for his old friends. It's your bid, Roberto."

"I pass."

"Then I will bid two dollars," said Julio, as the bid moved to him.

"Too rich for me," declared Sal. The others called the bet.

"How many cards do you want, Roberto?" asked Ben. Just then, the clock struck midnight.

All of the men looked at each other. "Uh oh,"

someone whispered. "It is after midnight." There was a pause in the hand as each man reflected upon the time. "We should wrap this up," said Ben.

"What? How am I supposed to get my money back?" cried Sal. He was a sore loser, as usual.

"You can get it back next time," declared Roberto. "Ben is right. We should not play cards after midnight."

"Well, we should at least finish this hand and then let everyone have one more deal around. That's only fair," declared Julio. "What do you say, Ben?"

"All right, but then we have to go. Roberto?"

"I'll stay, but I do not mind telling you that I have a funny feeling about this."

"Then let's just finish this hand now," said Ben and everyone turned back to his cards.

A knock at the door nearly made each man jump out of his skin. "Who would be visiting at this hour?" asked Julio as he rose to answer. He peered through the peephole and turned toward the others. "Why, it is Arturo! Hey, everyone! Art is here! Arturo has shown up after all!"

Julio opened the door and greeted his friend. "Art, you sly dog. I guess late is better than never. What kept you?"

Arturo did not reply. He just smiled and joined the other men at the table. They finished their hand and dealt Art in on the next round.

"So, Art, you are not talking too much this evening. Is everything all right with you?" asked Ben. "How is that beautiful wife of yours?"

Again, Arturo did not reply. He just smiled as he arranged the cards in his hand. He reached into his pocket and removed a five-dollar gold piece and placed it in the middle of the table as his wager.

"What is that?" asked Roberto. "I have never seen a five-dollar gold piece quite like it. Where did you get it?"

"From a card player!" replied the man, but it wasn't Art's voice at all. It was deep and sinister, and, as he said it, his face changed. All of Art's features began to melt into a wicked, dark-eyed creature that laughed and sneered at each of the players.

"Sweet Mary, it is the Devil!" Ben cried, jumping up from the table.

Everyone tried to get away. They fumbled and staggered in what would have been a funny scene if it weren't for the terror on their faces.

The Devil laughed and opened his arms to the men. "Come back, my friends. I love to play cards after midnight!"

Suddenly, Roberto got an idea. He quickly gathered up the cards and threw them in the fire. The flames crackled and spit, causing the Devil to shriek.

"What have you done? How dare you? I will not be tricked!" He started pacing the room, glaring at each man in turn. "You cannot win! I may have to go now, but I'll be back the next time you play cards after midnight! Next time, you will not get away!" With that, there was a big cloud of smoke. It circled each of the men and was then sucked up the chimney. The Devil was gone.

"So that's why your Papa never plays poker anymore, Raul?" asked Anna.

"That's what he says."

"But couldn't he play if he just didn't do it after midnight?" Anna was puzzled.

"I guess," interjected Marguerite. "But he says 'better safe than sorry.' So he prefers not to play at all."

"I'm scared," cried Anna. "I want to go to bed."

"Oh hush, Anna. There is nothing to be frightened of," said her brother.

"That's right," said Felix. "After all, we are not playing

poker and we are not drinking beer. We can play cards all night long." Felix laughed and winked at Raul. Manny gave them a "thumbs up" sign.

"But I thought the Devil said not to play *cards* after midnight. He didn't just say not to play poker," whined Anna. "Calm down, Anna," comforted Marguerite even as she glared at the boys. "They're just teasing you. It's an old story. Nobody really believes it anymore."

"Nana believes," Anna said quietly as she rubbed her sleeve across her nose, leaving a crusty snot mustache.

"That's because she is old, Anna. She can't help it. Old people always believe crazy stories. But you don't have to believe such nonsense."

"Manny, watch your mouth!" Sometimes Marguerite felt like she was the oldest instead of Manny. "Anna, sometimes elderly people still believe in stories from the old country. That doesn't mean they're crazy, just that they just haven't changed with the times. There are thousands of stories of the Devil in Old Mexico. But that is there, and we are here. You just have to remember that we live in modern times in an up-to-date country. You don't have anything to be afraid of."

"Okay, Marguerite, I understand," said Anna.

"Well, are we going to play Crazy 8s or what?" asked Raul.

"I'll play," said everyone except Anna. "I'll just watch," said Anna quietly.

"Scaredy-cat," teased Manny. All of the boys chuckled and poked at each other.

"Just deal the cards." Marguerite was tiring of their juvenile behavior. Before long, everyone started to enjoy the game, even Marguerite. Anna crept over to the breakfast nook, climbed up on a stool, and laid her head down on the counter. She was asleep before the next round.

WHAT WAS THAT? ANNA SAT UP SUDDENLY. HOW LONG HAD she been asleep? She felt confused and dazed. Someone was laughing. Within seconds, Anna breathed a sigh of relief. It was Marguerite's laugh that had awakened her.

"Hey guys, quit cheating!" Marguerite shouted playfully. She was laughing as she dealt the cards. "I know you can't play that good on your own!"

"What? You haven't heard? Manny and I are the masters of this game," declared Felix.

"You're the masters of something, all right. But I thought it was more the masters of what cows leave in the field," Raul teased.

"And what is that?" mocked Manny.

"He says we are the masters of cow poop!" declared Felix. Then he let out a huge fart. The boys laughed hysterically. Marguerite just shook her head.

Suddenly, Anna cried out. "Oh my gosh! Look at the clock!"

The time read 12:15. It was past midnight.

"I don't know why you had to scare her with that stupid story," Marguerite said to Raul. "You really frightened her."

"Yeah, now she'll never shut up so we can play. Anna, why don't you just go to bed?" asked her brother.

"But aren't you guys scared?"

"Oh, for crying out loud!" exclaimed Felix. "This is ridiculous. Anna, don't you understand? It is just an old story. Do you hear a knock at the door? Is there a stranger among us? Where is the Devil?"

"Here!" cried the Joker.

Suddenly, cards flew around the table in a ghastly ballet. The Joker stood straight up in the middle of the macabre card dance held just for his benefit. "I am here," it said as it stepped out of the card. "I've come to join your game!"

Anna started to scream, and the boys knocked over their chairs as they pushed themselves away from the table. Marguerite ran to Anna and held her.

"So you don't believe the old stories, right, Raul? And you, Manny, you think your sister should have more sense? I think I am lucky that foolish children like you still live in the world. Where else could I gather my lost souls?" The Devil Joker started to hop around the table. "Let's play cards! Let's play cards!"

Anna started to scream louder, and soon Marguerite and her brothers joined her. Only Manny remained calm. He was the oldest, and it was his job to take care of his sister and cousins. As he felt responsible, he knew it was his duty to act like a man.

"Joker Devil, you can't join us. We *quit* playing cards!" Manny was trying to distract the Joker.

"Pssst," hissed Raul. "Manny! Look!"

"Hush, Raul." Manny turned his attention back to the Joker Devil. "Didn't you hear me?" he asked. "I said, 'We *quit* playing.' Don't you think you should go?"

"Who are you to question the Devil?" roared the Joker. "I am the Ruler of the Underworld! Who are you?"

"He is my grandson!" shouted Nana as she snuck up behind the Joker. "He is mine, and so are the others!" Nana raised her Bible over her head and smacked the Joker flat on the table. "Quick!" she yelled. "Burn the cards in the sink!"

Manny gathered up the cards while Nana held the Bible on top of the Joker. He searched through the drawer for a match.

"Check the other drawer!" Nana shouted. It was getting hard to hold the Joker down. Marguerite started toward the table to help her, but Nana shouted for her to stay where she was. "Don't come any closer, *Mija*. I don't want him near you."

Manny rummaged through the drawer next to the sink and finally found some matches. The first one he struck sputtered and died without a flame.

"Hurry, Manny. Hurry!" cried his cousins.

"I am!"

Thankfully, as he struck a second match, it lit. Holding the flame up to one of the cards, it finally started to burn.

Then he tossed the card into the sink where the rest of the deck quickly caught fire. Within minutes the entire set was reduced to ashes, but the strange odor of charred flesh remained. Manny held up his hands. He wasn't burnt. So where was that stench coming from?

Everyone turned to look at Nana. She was standing with her Bible held close to her heart. The Joker had vanished. In his place was a smoldering fire and the blackened remains of evil.

Everyone learned a great lesson that night and remembered it throughout their lives. No one should play cards after midnight.

———

You see what I mean, *Mijos?* You must never doubt the old stories like we did when we were young. I saw the Joker Devil with my own *ojos*, my eyes. He almost took my cousins and my brother, Manny. I told this story to your Papa, and now I tell it to you. You must always remember it and tell your own children someday. *No debe jugar cartas después de la medianoche.* You must not play cards after midnight. Do not tempt the Devil to play with you!

12

EL BUS MEXICANO (THE MEXICAN BUS)

PASEOS GRATIS PARA TODOS - FREE RIDES FOR ALL

How COULD she take this anymore? Alma was ready to explode, or at least she felt that way. Good grief. Here she was, sixteen years old, and her parents still would not allow her to take the short walk of only nine miles to the neighboring village of Emiliano Zapata, deep in the jungle of Chiapas. Her community never held social events for young people, but Zapata held dances, meetings, and picnics just for teenagers. Ever since she turned thirteen, Alma had tried begging, crying, threatening, and even "the silent treatment," but her parents always nixed any idea she had regarding participation. Quite frankly, she was sick of it.

Maybe that's why Alma became so furious when her friend Antonia came by her house with news of yet another dance to be held the following weekend. According to Antonia, her parents and Pedro's parents had given their blessing to attend. Antonia suggested that maybe, since they would be in a group, Alma's parents would do the same. Alma successfully hid her irritation from her friend and said she would consider the idea.

Alma was less than enthusiastic about the proposition,

knowing all too well how angry her father had reacted the last time she approached him. She didn't think it was worth the effort if she met with that sort of verbal barrage just for asking. Somehow, however, Antonia had convinced her to try one more time.

Ugh. Alma had a pit in her stomach the size of Pico de Orizaba, the largest mountain in Mexico. Still, she willed herself to enter her own home and approach her parents, feeling like a deer about to enter a clearing where it was sure to be shot.

Standing quietly in a corner of the kitchen where Carlos and Yolanda, her parents, were discussing something, she became more and more agitated. Whatever the conversation topic, Alma had no idea, but she cleared her throat, making the noise to interrupt them

Both the adults turned her way, and Carlos, a puzzled look in his eyes, asked, "What do you want, *Mija*?"

Somewhat uncharacteristically, Alma held her head down, staring at the dirt floor, and asked, "Since Antonia and Pedro are going to the dance in Zapata, and we will be in a group, can I please go?"

Holding her breath, Alma scrunched her face and prepared for the onslaught she expected to come. Instead, she heard her mama say, "Our conversation was just about that very issue. We have spoken with Pedro's parents and Antonia's mother, and all of us decided to let you three go to the dance."

"Providing," interrupted her father, "that you all stay together and use some common sense. If any of you falter even once, the three of you will not go to another dance until you are adults. Do you understand?"

"*¡Sí*, Papa! *¡Sí!*" Alma was so happy, surprised, and overcome with emotion that she ran to her parents and hugged them both. All three agreed that it had been a long while since they had had no bickering in the home. This time was special, and Alma secretly congratulated herself for keeping her mouth shut and not ruining the moment.

Still, Alma had to break the jovial family embrace and hurry to find her friends. She couldn't wait to tell them her news!

Once outside in the courtyard of the small village where they all lived, Alma spotted her cohorts standing against a wall of a small market. "I can go!" she screamed. "I can go!"

Both Antonia and Pedro laughed and informed her that they had known it all along. Their parents had simply made them vow not to share the news with her until Alma's parents could give her the information. All three teenagers were jumping and laughing and holding each other in great celebration. Finally, they were able to settle down and start making plans. It was only Tuesday, but they had to be ready for this glorious event by Saturday. Let the delightful planning begin!

First, of course, the young ladies had to discuss their apparel for Saturday night, and Pedro was tasked with judging the fashion show as the girls exhibited prospective outfits. They began at Antonia's house, where she subjected both of her friends to nearly ninety minutes of garment evaluation as she modeled each choice. Both Pedro and Alma were somewhat peeved when the final decision turned out to be the third possibility from the beginning of the style spectacle, but Alma wasn't about to show her aggravation because it was finally her turn to model. Unfortunately, because Antonia had taken so long, the three friends had to postpone Alma's exhibition until the next day.

Alma was disappointed, but the following day arrived quickly, and Alma met her friends at her home. She sat them down in the tiny living room, better described as a family room, and went into a makeshift bedroom her father had made for her when she had reached puberty. From there she could dress herself and then dramatically open her door (well, it was a curtain) and with a dramatic flourish, make a grand entrance when she stepped into the room where her friends waited. Antonia and Pedro played along by clapping, whistling, and making "ooohs and ahhhs" like they were real fashion critics at a big city show. It was fun!

The show didn't last long, however, because Alma didn't have that many choices for what she could wear. Her friend, Antonia, declared that all of Alma's outfits were lovely, but she could, if she wanted, borrow something from Antonia's closet. Pedro thought Alma might be offended, but the result was just the opposite. They scrambled out the door and scurried toward Antonia's house, where Alma picked out a black and red dress that looked fabulous when she tried it on. Settled. That was what she would wear, and everyone was ecstatic. After all, Pedro didn't really have to worry at all. His choice turned out to be his church clothes, and that was that. He just wanted the girls to be pleased for themselves.

Finally, the day of this spectacular opportunity arrived. Alma was so excited she hadn't really slept at all the night before. By Saturday afternoon, when Pedro and Antonia came to "pick her up" for the walk, she was ready to sprint all the way. Pedro warned her, however, that running would just make her look tired and disheveled, so it would be best to just walk at a brisk pace.

"How long is this going to take?" Alma asked.

"About an hour and a half," came the reply from Antonia. "That's why we need to leave now!" It was clear that Antonia was just as excited as Alma. "The dance starts at 6 o'clock. Let's go! Let's go!"

"I am almost ready," proclaimed Alma. It was 4:30 in the afternoon, but she had been ready since a few minutes after the noon hour. She just couldn't settle down and was fidgety and nervous for hours. "Pedro, could you help me carry my good shoes and my purse?"

Pedro revealed a backpack he had fashioned from a feed bag. "I figured both of you would want help." Of course, he was correct, and the girls were very happy to have him carry their extra weight.

By 4:35, the threesome was actually out the door and on their way. Alma's mother called out to all of them as they skipped down the path. "Remember to follow the rules! You must be home by midnight!"

The friends turned and waved, shouting promises to do just as their parents had insisted. They would leave the festivities by 10:30 and be home right on time. No problem.

As they made their way toward Zapata, each of the three friends found the going was quite easy. Walking was the way of life in their village, so the trip went by quickly, especially because they could talk and laugh all along the journey. What fun!

When the group arrived in Zapata, it wasn't difficult to find the location of the revelry. All they had to do was follow the seemingly hundreds of other teenagers to the center of town, where they found all types of decorations. *Piñatas*, elaborate decorations of cut paper called *papel picado*, and Huichol bead masks were everywhere. Torches surrounded the town square, giving plenty of light even though the sun was slowly making way for the moon to take its place. It was breathtaking to Alma.

Everywhere the friends gazed, they found unexpected delights. For instance, Zapata's town council had set up refreshment stations, games, and activities all around the dance area. Thank goodness Alma's parents had given her some *pesos* to spend. Nothing was expensive, but there were charges to play games or partake of the food or drink. Alma thought she only wanted to dance, but after a while, the lemonade sure tasted great.

As for the dancing, the girls had shared reservations that they may only be asked by Pedro, but that wasn't the case at all. All the boys from Zapata seemed to enjoy the new faces and dance partners, and the local girls were welcoming as well. It was a fabulous time for all.

As the clock in the town square approached 10:30 p.m., the threesome knew it was time to start making their good-byes. Each of them were thrilled to hear that another Teenage Night was scheduled for the following month, and everyone asked if they would come. New friends, new activities, new surroundings…Pedro, Antonia, and Alma couldn't be happier. They promised they would attend the next gathering. In fact, they could hardly wait.

One might think that the group would be tired on the long walk back home, but this was not the case. Each friend was so excited and wound up that they chattered and giggled the entire way home. Alma couldn't believe how fast the time went.

Pedro and Antonia dropped Alma off first. As she said her good-byes, she rushed into her house to find and embrace both her mother and father. She was excited to tell them all about her evening. That was a shock to everyone, as Alma was usually quiet and didn't want to share her life experiences with anyone in the family. This time was different. Babbling on until almost 1 a.m., Alma gave extensive details about the evening and reveled in the night's happenings with her parents. Her mother and father let her go on, because they were touched to have her acting as close to them as she was as a younger child. Everyone was happy in their household and didn't want to break the spell.

Right before Alma petered out, she told her parents about the upcoming Teen Night the following month. Her mother was especially happy and gave her permission to attend right away. As the young Alma made her way to her bed, she in fact sang one of the songs she had heard earlier that night. What a blissful spell! Alma was able to fall asleep almost immediately.

THE NEXT DAY, WHICH WAS ACTUALLY THE SAME DAY DUE TO the hour that she went to bed, Alma was pleasantly surprised that her parents, in fact, had let her sleep in. Instead of early Mass, they attended afternoon church service as a family, each of them basking in a glow that had been absent since Alma was much younger. They were a cheerful household, and when they came across Pedro's and Antonia's parents, who also came to the later church service, the adults seemed content to speak among themselves while the teens had their own huddled summit. The grownups were obviously pleased knowing that their children had a good time and came back in much better spirits than they had exhibited prior to the outing. The young adults were just as pleased to have been given more freedom and trust. It was a situation where all felt they were the winners.

So it was decided. Next month, the threesome could once again go to the neighboring village. No one had any objections.

Time seemed to crawl at a snail's pace for the group of friends. All three were equally excited about the next festival.

They chattered on and on about it, creating a cacophony

of delight as the other students at their school tried to ask questions. The ugly head of envy and jealousy never even reared its head. Other students, younger than they, were simply able to savor the air of glee and anticipation.

FINALLY, THE DAY OF THE NEXT FESTIVAL ARRIVED, AND THE three friends went through the exact same routine as they had done for the previous visit. The only difference was that the girls simply couldn't wear the same dress as before, so a new fashion show was held, and Antonia and Alma were quite pleased to alter their style statements.

When the threesome arrived in Zapata, Alma thought they would simply hang together as had been the case for their previous visit. However, there was no repeat of the experience from last month. Instead, Antonia and Pedro went separate ways, so Alma was pretty much left to her own devices. Luckily, there were friends she had made from before, so Alma was happy and felt no worry. She still had fun, and plenty of it.

Regrettably, time flashed by very quickly, and the three friends were late getting back together for their journey home. Even with a brisk pace, they were still late for their return and hoped their parents would understand. They understood, all right, but each of them was restricted from attending the next event on the calendar. Luckily, they only had to miss one event, and on the second month, their parents allowed them to attend again. Of course, the parents gave a loud warning that if their return was after midnight for a second time, there would be no further attendance ever or "as long as you live in my house."

Alma had no reservation about the requirement of a

midnight deadline. She was simply excited and content that she had permission to go at all. Her intention was to return a little earlier to reassure her parents, and she believed that Pedro and Antonia felt the same way, but that was not the case.

As the hour of ten came and went, Alma could find neither of her friends, and she became quite worried. Finally, around eleven p.m., they approached her in the courtyard.

"Alma, we're sorry we left you alone, but we have decided to stay," declared Antonia.

"Stay?" gasped Alma. "What do you mean by that?"

Pedro answered. "We talked about it and realized that we have more fun here. We are going to spend the night."

"What!?!" screamed Alma. "Do you realize they will never let us come back if we pull that stunt!"

"Don't worry," said Antonia in a calm voice. "We will come up with an excuse. Everything will be fine."

"Oh, my God," screeched Alma. "This can't be happening. I am going home. If I have to do it alone, well that's perfect. I should have never trusted you in the first place," she pouted.

"Please, Alma," begged Pedro. "Just stay with us!"

"No! I am going home even if I have to walk alone." With that declaration, Alma set out toward her their native village. She certainly wasn't thrilled with the prospect of walking by herself, but anything was better than the wrath of her parents. Confidence was a trait she nourished in herself, and she pretended to have a bucket full of it when she set out.

Alma's hearty conviction didn't last long, of course. As soon as she left the safety of the glow of Zapata's torches and lights, she began to doubt her decision. The road home was gloomy, really shadowy, and scary. Worst of all, she had to hurry because she was starting half an hour late. That made the trip even more frightening.

To add insult to injury, Alma forgot to retrieve her walking shoes from Pedro's makeshift backpack. Navigating the mountain roads in her high heels was difficult in the light of day. Nighttime without a moon made it nearly impossible, but Alma was determined and trudged away the best she could.

After what she thought was about an hour, Alma heard a strange rumbling from behind her and turned around to see what was approaching. It was a a huge, gray bus she had never seen before. The driver pulled up beside her and with a "swoosh" opened the door to speak with her.

"*Señorita*, do you want a ride? I can take you to where you are going. Step inside." The driver had a strange aura, and his face was pasty white. He looked like an actor ready for a stage production, covered in makeup and sporting a lewd smile.

Alma just stared at him, as she was unable to form a response.

"*Sí, Señorita*. The ride on my bus is free. I come to help young people on their way. Just come aboard." His mustache, large and hairy, bobbed up and down as he spoke. All of his mannerisms made him look like a puppet, a very scary marionette.

Alma stuttered but was finally able to voice an answer. "No, no thank you. I cannot take a ride. My parents would kill me if I accepted assistance from a stranger."

"But I am no stranger, my Sweet. I am a bus driver. It is my responsibility to help young people get to where they are going." Again, the hairy caterpillar on his lip jumped and wiggled as he spoke.

"Thank you, anyway. I will walk," Alma declared with more conviction that she felt.

"Okay," the bus driver replied with a slow shake of his head. "Do as you please." With that, the driver pulled on ahead of Alma. On the side of the vehicle, Alma saw fancy lettering that read, Mexican Bus. *Paseos gratis para todo -* Free rides for all," but the words are not really what caught her eye.

What actually grabbed Alma's attention was the view above the signage. There, Alma saw her friend, Antonia, pounding on the window and apparently screaming, though Alma could hear no words. As her hands pounded on the clear space, streaks of blood started to seep down and cover the view. Frantically, Antonia seemed to be saying "Help me!" and she was crying, weeping actually, and pulling her own hair by the roots.

Then Alma saw Pedro, acting much in the same was as Antonia. She tried to yell so they could hear her, but Alma felt helpless. The bus driver simply drove off, leaving her to give chase to help her friends. Of course, there was no way to catch up, and the vehicle was quickly swallowed by the darkness ahead.

Alma kicked off her shoes and started to run. Her feet became raw and bloodied, but she kept sprinting as fast as she could.

When Alma finally reached her home, the bus was nowhere to be found. Her parents were prepared to have a gigantic battle, but saw that Alma was shrieking and bawling and crying. Rather than fight, they talked with their daughter. What they heard was ear-piercing, and they, too, had to screech just to force Alma to stop. Once everyone was able to control the shattering noise, Alma was able to explain.

"Mama! Papa! Pedro and Antonia wanted to stay overnight, so I decided to walk back alone."

"Alone?!? What do you mean by 'alone?' How could this happen? We told you never to walk alone!" shouted her father.

"Please, my husband," whispered her mama. "We need to hear what Alma has to say."

Alma continued to explain, but when she arrived at the part of her tale detailing the bus, the driver, the words she read on the side, and, of course, Antonia and Pedro, poor Alma could hardly get the words out without crying and grabbing her mama.

Alma's parents sat listening with wide, shocked eyes that looked like jack-o'-lanterns. Fear enveloped the entire family and gave way to sadness.

"I have to go and talk with the other parents," said Alma's father. "We need to go look for those kids. *Mija*, I am proud of you for refusing to enter that bus. Settle down now. Your mama will sit with you while I go and make a search."

Before long, Alma and her mother were sitting with Antonia's mother and Pedro's mama and *tía*, his aunt. None of the women had words for what they felt. It was a silent vigil, waiting to hear news, the only sound being the whispered prayers recited by all.

Unfortunately, there were no reports. The men scoured the road to Zapata but found no trace of the missing friends. They never did, and villagers included the two lost teenagers in their prayers for decades.

Alma was unable to ever quite recover. For the rest of her days, she mourned her friends. She also would not leave her village, even to visit family or friends. Terrified that she might once again see the bus, Alma ended her days alone in her house, a sad old lady who could not forget her past.

Mijita, this is *un historia triste*, a sad story. You must always *recordar*, remember. *Sí*, you can never take a ride from a stranger, that is true, but also, you must follow the rules of your Mama and Papa. No, do not think you know best! I heard this very story from my *abuela*, as I now tell you. Do not make your parents cry. No, you do not want to be a passenger on *el Bus Mexicano*, the Mexican Bus!

13

TATA'S CHAIR

I WAS VERY LITTLE when my grandparents came to live with us. In fact, I don't actually remember a time when they didn't stay in the back bedroom of our ranch- style house. Mama told me they came from Mexico to live with us and be closer to their grandchild. I think they came to be closer to Mama. They loved Mama very much, and she adored them. We were a happy family because love lived in our house.

I called them Nana and Tata. Nana was a beautiful woman with long black hair, streaked with white, that she kept pulled back and rolled into a bun. She told me it didn't get in her way if she kept it drawn back. That was important, because Nana was always busy doing something around the house. Mama said she had the energy of a young girl. I didn't know what energy was, but I knew that Nana had something special. I loved her.

I worshipped Tata, a big man who smiled and laughed often. He smoked a brown, silver-tipped pipe and sat in his favorite rocker while telling funny stories about his past. I used to sit with him in that rocker for hours on end.

Sometimes Mama would take a seat on the floor at his

feet, and he would keep us laughing throughout the evening. Nana would always sit next to him in her own rocker and add comments as he went along. Papa would sprawl out on the couch and sometimes fall asleep, but he loved the stories, too. He once told me that he hoped that someday he would have as many stories to tell his grandchildren. We all loved the tales, and we all loved Tata.

That's why it was such a shock the morning Papa came into my room with the bad news.

"*Mijita*, I have something to tell you." I noticed his eyes were red and he looked like he had not slept at all. "Tata died last night. He has gone to heaven."

"No, Papa. Tata is in his room sleeping. He is not in heaven."

"No, *Mijita*. He is gone. The people came for him just a few minutes ago. They will bring his body back tomorrow, and he will rest in our front room for two days. Then we will bury him, but his soul is in heaven now."

I ran past my father's embrace and went through the house to my Nana and Tata's room. Crashing through the door, I cried out, "Where's Tata?"

Nana sat on the bed, looking much older than I had remembered her. She was crying, and her hair was down on her shoulders instead of pulled back in a bun. As she looked up, her arms opened, inviting me to crawl into her lap.

"Come here, *Mijita*."

I ran to Nana and buried my face in the soft folds of her dress. "Nana, I don't understand. Where is my Tata?" I burst into tears.

Nana stroked my hair and held me tight. When my sobbing finally subsided, she started to explain.

"*Mijita, tu Tata seha ido con Dios.* How you say? Oh. I remember now. Your Tata has gone to be with God. I know that it makes us sad right now, but we must be brave. Your Tata would have wanted it that way. Just remember, he is gone from us, but he waits for us in heaven. Someday, we will all be together again."

"But I don't want to die, Nana. I want to stay here with you and Mama and Papa!" I cried in dismay.

"*Mijita*, you are not going to die now. You will live a long and wonderful life with many children of your own, and I hope you will tell your *niños* all about your Tata and his stories. But there must come a time for all of us to go to Heaven. My time will come sooner than yours. *Mi preciosa nieta*, you have a long life to live."

"But Nana, I don't want you to go, either!"

"Don't worry, *Mijita*. I will be with you for a while yet."

She kept stroking my hair for a long time as we sat in silence. When I looked up, I realized that Papa was standing at the door. He walked into the room and bent down to kiss Nana on the cheek. Without another word, he picked me up and carried me out of the room. I rested my head on his shoulders and did not speak. I was too sad to talk anymore.

THE NEXT DAY, THE MEN BROUGHT TATA'S BODY BACK. HE was lying in a big open box on shiny white pillows and lining. They put the box with Tata in the living room on a long table. I was terrified to go anywhere near him because he looked strange without the smile on his face. There was no getting around the fact that I was afraid.

But not Mama. As soon as the men left, she raced into the living room and pulled a chair up next to Tata. My Mama sat there all day, talking to her Papa. Sometimes when I looked in I would see her crying and pleading for something. Other times, she just sat silent while she held his hand. But I never saw her leave. She stayed there all day, and maybe all night, too. I don't really know for sure, because Papa told me not to bother her. He said she was very upset and needed this time with Tata. Confused and depressed, I didn't understand. Wasn't Tata supposed to be in heaven? Why was she talking to him in the living room? I was frightened and very unhappy.

The days passed very slowly. People kept dropping in, and they would go to sit with Mama in the room with Tata. Nana went in, too, but she didn't stay there all the time like Mama. Nana got up and fixed meals or put away the food that the neighbors brought. It was all very baffling for me. Everyone seemed too busy or sad to spend time with me. I spent as much time in my room as possible, trying to forget what was happening in my house.

On the second night after Tata was moved into our living room, Papa came to my room and sat on my bed.

"*Mijita*, tomorrow we will have Tata's funeral. We will go to the church and then we will take Tata's body to the cemetery. He will be buried there in a special spot. It will be a hard time for your Nana and your Mama, so you must be very good at the service. Afterward, everything will be better, I am sure. I will help you to get ready in the morning so you will look your best."

"Papa, why doesn't Mama help me? She hasn't even come in to see me for three days."

"*Mijita*, Mama is very sad right now. All she wants to do it sit with Tata. I am sure she will get better after the funeral tomorrow. Now go to sleep and get some rest. Tomorrow is a big day."

Papa turned off my light as he shut the door. I could hear

people talking in the house throughout the night. It took a long time, but I was finally able to fall asleep.

———————

IN THE MORNING, PAPA FED ME BREAKFAST AND THEN HELPED me dress in my Sunday church dress. I wanted to ask him more questions, but he looked so sad that I thought it would be best if I just kept quiet.

When we rode to the church with our neighbor, I sat on Papa's lap. I wanted to sit with Mama, but she was crying and sobbing, and I was afraid of her. Papa kept telling me that everything was going to be all right. That made me feel a little better.

I do not remember very much from the funeral, except for one part. It was bad. In the middle of the service, my Mama jumped up from her seat and ran up to the box where Tata lay resting. Mama was crying and screaming, and she begged Tata not to leave her. Papa had to go up and drag Mama back to her seat. The church was very quiet afterward, but I could hear many people crying and sniffling. Everyone was very sad.

After the church service, we went to the cemetery. There, Tata's box was placed in the ground and people came by and threw handfuls of dirt on the top. Papa wanted me to throw some dirt, but I screamed and ran to Nana. She shook her head at Papa and held me very close while people filed by. I just could not do what they were doing. No way was I going to throw dirt on top of Tata. Nana understood.

Mama waited until last and then threw a red flower down into the hole with Tata. Afterward, she turned very quickly and left. Papa and I had to almost run to catch up with her.

Nana stayed behind with my Tía and Tío who had come in from California. Sadness showed on everyone's face.

We rode back home with our neighbor. It was a quiet trip.

No one said a word. I think I fell asleep in Papa's lap.

When we arrived at our house, Mama ran in ahead of us. Papa stayed behind to thank the neighbor, who said he would return in a short while with more food for the family.

Suddenly, we heard Mama scream, and Papa flew through the front door. I followed as fast as I could.

Mama was sitting in the living room, laughing and crying at the same time. The table where the box had been was gone, and our furniture was back in place. Mama sat on the couch, pointing at Tata's chair.

"Look, Francisco! Look," she said to Papa. "He has returned! My Papa did not leave me!" She pointed to Tata's chair. It was rocking back and forth, just as it had done when he sat in it to tell us stories.

"What is that smell?" I asked.

"It is the smell of his pipe!" Mama shouted. "He has come back!" Those were the first words she had spoken to me in days, but they did not make me feel better. I was more scared than ever. Mama had a wild look in her eyes, and I clung to Papa's leg with all my strength.

Just then, the door opened and Nana came in with my Tía and Tío. Mama jumped up and ran to her. "Mama, he has come back." She showed Nana the chair and asked her if she could smell the pipe.

Nana looked unhappy. She did not smile like Mama. She grabbed her heart and Papa and Tío had to help her into her room. As they led her down the hall, Nana looked back at Mama. "*Mija*, you have done *una cosa muy mala*, a very bad thing. Your father needs to go to his rest. It is very bad, *muy mala*."

"No, Mama," my Mama replied. "It is good. Now he will be with us always."

"Oh, *Mija*." Nana just shook her head as Papa and Tío helped her into her room.

Tía went to Mama and tried to get her to sit down, but people started arriving from the cemetery, and Mama went to greet them. She told everyone that Tata had returned, and some of them shook their heads and went to speak with Tía or Papa, but most of them looked at Mama, turned, and left right away. No one seemed happy like Mama.

I wasn't happy. Instead, I was more frightened than ever. Confused, I thought that once Tata was put in the cemetery, Mama would start taking care of me again. It didn't happen. Instead, she seemed to be in her own little world. My memories of that time are of loneliness, helpless to change anything whatsoever.

DAYS WENT BY, THEN MONTHS. THEN A STRANGE phenomenon happened. I can't even tell you when it began, but slowly Mama came back to me. Happiness began to creep back into our lives as I found myself sitting on Mama's lap in the evenings, and going to town with her in the days. Our house had been so sad for so long that it felt wonderful to have these little times of happiness.

Before I knew it, our lives seemed back to normal. Mama loved me again, and she would smile and tell stories just like the old days, except for one difference. Mama would not tell stories about Tata, and eventually, she would not go into the living room at all. Tata's chair still rocked at strange times, and Mama seemed to be afraid of it. If the smell of his pipe was in the house, she would run outside. When this happened, Mama did not seem happy, but she was fine when it didn't.

Unfortunately, Tata started coming more often about a year after he died. It seemed like his chair was rocking every night, and the smell of his pipe always lingered in the house. Mama became more and more unhappy. Sometimes she would come in from the yard and start crying again, or she would shout at me for no reason. I started to be afraid again.

Then Nana decided to fix everything. I was standing in the kitchen when I heard her call Mama to her room. I followed Mama down the hall, but stood outside the door to hear what Nana had to say.

"Mija, what you have done is wrong. You begged and pleaded with your Papa's soul to stay with you, and now he thinks he cannot leave. You must tell him, *Mija*, tell him you do not need him. Tell him you do not want him. It is up to you to convince him to go."

"But how can I do that?" Mama cried.

"You must find a way. He stayed for you. Now he must leave for you."

Mama laid her head on Nana's lap and cried. I felt very sorry for both of them, so I left the doorway and went into the living room where Tata's chair was rocking. I walked straight to the seat and climbed up into it as it rocked. It felt very cold sitting there, even though it was a warm day, but I just held my arms around myself and started talking out loud to Tata.

"Tata, you know that we all love you. Nana and Mama were very sad when you died. But life is getting better now. Mama isn't so sad anymore, and she has started to spend time with me again. She cannot spend time with you. You have to go."

I looked up and saw Mama and Nana standing in the hall. Mama came over to me and picked me up. I felt her shudder as she sensed the cold. She kissed me and then started to speak.

"Papa, Elena is right. It is time for you to go. I thought I wanted you to stay forever, but I was wrong. It is making me crazy having you here. I need to spend my time with the living, and I need you to go. You have to go!" Mama broke down into tears.

"Enrique, do as your daughter and granddaughter have asked," Nana added. "I know you loved us, but it is time for you to go. Wait for me in heaven. I will see you there soon."

Mama cried even louder, and then a strange thing happened. The chair suddenly quit rocking. It didn't slow down, just stopped. Then Mama looked up. "Goodbye, Papa," she whispered. Nana came over and put her arms around both of us.

Mama began crying, then Nana started crying. I wanted to make them feel better, so I said, "Don't cry. Tata is happy now. You should be happy, too. Now we can have our living room back."

Both Mama and Nana started laughing through their tears. Then they kissed me and Mama put me down. "Let's go start dinner," Mama said. We all went into the kitchen.

That was the last time Tata's chair rocked without a person in it. Well, almost the last time. There was one other. It happened three years later, right after Nana died. We were very sad, but Mama seemed to be able to handle the situation better this time. Oh, she still cried, but she seemed to understand this time that Nana was in a better place.

The incident with the chair happened after Nana's funeral. When we got back to the house, Mama went into the living room, and we heard her gasp. Papa and I ran to see what was the matter. We found her standing in the middle of the room looking at Tata and Nana's chairs. Both of them were rocking! Suddenly, the chairs stopped, and we all felt cold, cold air around us. But the funny point was, the air didn't feel bad. Instead, it felt like love. It circled us for a moment, and then it was gone.

"They just said goodbye," Papa said. "I know," whispered Mama.

"And they said they love us," I said. I looked up and shouted, "We love you, too!" Then we went out to greet our visitors.

YOU SEE, *MIJITA*, YOU HAVE TO LET THE DEAD GO. MY MAMA learned that the hard way. Remember, though, that you don't have to forget those who go on to *el cielo*, to heaven.

That is why we honor those like Nana and Tata on *El Día de los Muertos*, the Day of the Dead. We visit their graves so they will know that we remember them. I want them to know that I told my Nana's and Tata's stories to my children and now to you, my grandchild.

Someday, I will join them *en el cielo*, in heaven. I do not want you to be sad. Just think of me, and remember that you, too, must tell the stories. *Eso me hará feliz*. That will make me happy. Then, one day, we all be together in heaven. We will all be happy, and our stories will live on.

AFTERWORD

ABOUT THE AUTHOR AND THE ORIGIN OF THESE TALES

Diane Willsey (aka Diane Riggs and Diane Stuckey) – that's me – was born and raised in Tucson, Arizona. Even though I lived with Mexican American friends all my life, I actually never heard most of these tales until I became an adult. My first contact with Mexican Folklore came when I started as a Music/Art/Whatever Teacher in Altar Valley, west of Tucson, back in 1984. It was there that students started coming and sharing scary stories from their own families. As time went on, I heard many of the same stories (each with a different twist) from my writing students in Marana, just north of Tucson. That is when I first realized that my students and their families had a treasure trove of fabulous legends and anecdotes, and most of them came from the matriarch of the families, the Mexican Grandmothers. With all due respect, I encouraged my students to talk with these women and bring their stories to our classrooms. Years later, I was able to put the tales into my own words and scenarios while keeping true to the original lessons. And yes, they all have lessons!

I am sometimes asked what makes these tales mine. That's easy. I have heard dozens of versions of some of these, but you will never see or hear my versions except from me. That's because I based my theme and topic on the folklore, but I added my own settings and development of the story lines. I also enjoyed the opportunity to include some events from my own life. Yes, my mother *did* sit and wait in a dark living room when I stayed out too late. Sure enough, she always scared me silly when I thought I had made it inside. My father also *did* come to my bedroom door and pound on it, saying, "You're sleeping your life away!" And yes, I did go with my boyfriend to A Mountain and "check out the scenery." Pretty much everything comes from me except the core of each story, the values carried on by Mexican Grandmothers. My biggest compliments have come from these same grandmothers when they tell me I have written it "just right" or when I would read aloud and my students would laugh and declare, "You sound just like my Nana!" I was privileged to hear the stories and even more honored to be able to share my versions.

So, from where did these stories come? Here are some anecdotal notes:

1. The Club Diablo.

I used to call these stories "Chicken Feet" because that was the one constant. Every year I would do a family and community history project in my classroom, and every year I would hear a variation of this tale. The location might change, but the gist of the story always remained the same. I even had a young man tell me that his grandmother told him the devil was a woman with chicken feet (trying to keep him in line!). One year, my students made a Haunted House for the school carnival and frightened the visitors by using real chicken feet to touch them asthey walked through. I loved their ingenuity and the fact that they were able to bring something from their family histories to our present-day scary situation. Eventually, I heard that the story can be found in Mexico dating back to the 1850s. The lesson? Don't disobey your parents or cavort (dance) with strangers! It is still relevant today, don't you agree?

2. El Cucuy.

Once I was in a groove with my writing, I wanted to increase the number of stories I could share. El Cucuy was my first tale strictly from research.

This one comes mostly from exploration via the internet, though I did have a few students who remembered the creature after I read it aloud to them. Basically, El Cucuy is the Mexican Boogeyman, told to children to get them to go to sleep!

3. La Llorona.

I wonder if there is anyone in Arizona, New Mexico, Colorado, or Old Mexico who doesn't know a story of La Llorona, who is known across all of these areas. The backstory of how her child or children came to die in a river often changes, but the point remains the same. Children need to stay away from a river, as it can surge in a flash flood and carry youngsters away. The Santa Cruz River in Tucson has been dry for many years, but it still can rise in a flash flood and become quite dangerous.

4. El Chupacabra.

We have all heard stories of the Goat Suckers, at least where I come from. You can find newspaper articles on this topic as well, especially when herds of goats were found dead in Puerto Rico in the 1990s. The first time I told my son about El Chupacabra, we were terrified when we heard some sort of animal try to enter our family room via the pet door immediately after I finished the account! Of course, the lesson to be learned is to never go out into the desert at night, especially alone. Just good sense if you ask me.

5. La Mujer De Blanco.

When I first started hearing about this phenomenon, I thought it was just a version of La Llorona. I was mistaken. This is another of the most prevalent stories I heard, and they all had one important fact in common: a bar and drinking alcohol. That, I believe, is the point. Don't go out drinking, as well as stay faithful to your wife. Just another piece of good advice in my eyes!

6. La Mano Peluda.

I have only heard a few varieties of this folktale. In fact, most of them are only, "If you tell your mama you hate her, the Hairy Hand will get you!" I liked that, so the first time I heard it, I went home and told my own children, who will attest to this day that I scared the dickens out of them. Of course, they never told me they hated me, that's for sure.

7. Bloody Mary.

I heard this story when I was growing up but never realized that it was so popular even today. This was a wonderful opportunity for me to elaborate. No one could ever tell me exactly what Bloody Mary looked like or why she appeared. I made up my own version. However, I did hear a story about a re-appearing Ouija Board!

8. Jackpot!

Seriously, when casinos first came to Tucson in the 1990s, I heard many a twisted tale of the Devil being seen at one of our local establishments. I believe there was even a newspaper article attesting

9. The Tlahuelpuchi.

This is a story found through internet research. When I began to explore my students' stories, I came across more tales like this. Should you want to explore also, I suggest you do a search for **Tlahuelpuchi.** You are now forewarned that if you do this search, expect to spend a great deal of time at your computer. The choices of information are seemingly endless. In addition, you may enjoy reading about *Panteón de Belén*. It is a real cemetery in Guadalajara, Mexico. Dig deeper and you can also discover a tomb for a child built above ground, as well as a shadow of a hanging child. One note I did not include in my story was a video account of women killing an owl, trying to make it return to its human form (a witch). You can find a great amount of information, but not all of it is pretty.

10. El Hombre Cabra De La Montaña "A".

I first heard this narrative from a friend of mine. I was fascinated because A Mountain is a hangout for every teenager in Tucson, at least it was in my time. The mountain has a large painted A, for the University of Arizona. My friend told me that the Goat Man lived in a cave with bars on the front somewhere on the mountain. He also said the cave is there from the days that dynamite was kept to blast the roadway that eventually was built to allow access to the view. I have never seen the cavern, but my friend insists it is there, and that the Goat Man uses it as his home to this day. Again, why tell this tale? To keep your granddaughter (or son) from going to A Mountain where teenagers "neck" or "make out" as we called it.

11. El Cucuy.

Once I was in a groove with my writing, I wanted to increase the number of stories I could share. El Cucuy was my first tale strictly from research.

This one comes mostly from exploration via the Internet, though I did have a few students who remembered the creature after I read it aloud to them. Basically, El Cucuy is the Mexican Boogieman, told to children to get them to go to sleep!

12. El Bus Mexicano.

Here is another story found on the internet via Mexican Urban Legends (Scary Stories for Kids: Mexican Urban Legends: http://www.scaryforkids.com/urban-legends/.) For some reason, this bus story resonated with me, so I developed it into the account you read today. The way I came up with the idea for the story line was merely my own instinct and the different tales I heard from grandmothers of all nationalities about following your parents' guidance and do as you're told!

13. Tata's Chair.

I believe this the best story I have ever written simply for the emotional aspect. I have heard different versions, but what prompted this was a conversation I had with the school secretary at a school where I worked. Her father had recently passed away, and he had been a joker, a funny man, in the family. Even after he died, the jokes continued. When I gave my friend my earliest attempt to write the story, she cried. Honestly, I also cry every time I read it.

It was my pleasure to read these stories out loud to my students every year for over twenty years. Now, it is my honor to offer them to readers of all ages. I hope you have enjoyed them and will share them. That was always my intent.

Have a scary story yourself? I would love to hear it! Feel free to write to me at Diane.Willsey55@gmail.com.

I would love to hear from any and all!

ABOUT KYDALA PUBLISHING, INC,

Kydala Publishing, Inc. runs BundleRabbit.com, the premier DIY ebook bundling and royalty splitting publishing service. BundleRabbit allows collaborative publishing of ebooks and paperbacks across every major digital platform in one consolidated dashboard. For more information visit www.bundlerabbit.com.

Made in the USA
Monee, IL
30 November 2023

47803086R00105